JTF

James T. Farrell

This Man and

This Woman

The Vanguard Press, Inc.   New York

To Lillian and Jack Farrell

1

It's just like you to bring home a present I have no use for," Peg Callahan said acidly.

"But I'm sure we can use it," Walt answered earnestly.

They were having supper. Peg had cooked frankfurters and beans. Walt leaned forward and continued eating.

Walt Callahan was a tall and rather thin man of sixty-three, with graying hair, a wearied, kindly face, and soft, blue eyes. His skin was roughened and weather-beaten. Sitting with his shirt sleeves rolled up, he looked content and mellow. Peg was tall and thin, too. She was fifty-three and had straight, black hair just beginning to turn gray, and dark, intense eyes. Her face was beginning to show its age; her cheeks were slightly sunken, and there were wrinkles and hollows under her eyes. Her fingers were long and talonlike. She was sloppy-looking in an old black dress.

"Of all the things to buy," she said.

Walt glanced at her appealingly.

"How did you even happen to think of bringing something home?"

"Oh, I noticed it in a drugstore window on Van

Buren Street, and I . . . well . . . I thought it would be a nice kind of a little gadget to have in the house, and we can save money with it, too. On hot nights, if we want root beer instead of beer, we can make our own, and when Dorothy and Jack are here with the kids we can make root beer for them. And you used to like to make desserts with whipped cream, and, Peg, you can make whipped cream out of just plain ordinary cream with this Little Gem Syphon."

"Now that you've bought it, you won't use it twice in a year. It seems to me that there were plenty of more practical things you could have thought of to buy."

"But, Peg—"

"You wouldn't think of bringing home something for me, would you?"

A hurt, boyish expression crossed his face.

"But I did bring this for you, for the home, Peg. I thought you'd like it."

"Yes, and I suppose it will cause me twice as much trouble as it will be worth."

"Well, Peg, if you feel that way about it, I can take it back and get something else. Tell me something you'd like, and I'll bring it home to you tomorrow night."

She didn't answer him. He sat with his fork poised, waiting.

"But, Peg, is there something else I can get you? Tell me if there's anything you'd rather have for the house or for yourself instead of this Little Gem Syphon, and I'll get it."

"You wanted this useless piece of junk, keep it."

"But if you don't want it, Peg—"

"What does it matter what I want?" she asked disconsolately.

Walt looked puzzled.

"But, Peg, what's the matter?" he asked solicitously.

"Oh, nothing, nothing's the matter. I suppose I expected too much of you. Maybe it's just the way of expressmen. Maybe no expressman ever thinks much of his wife."

"But I do think of you, Peg. I did when I bought this present, this . . . Little Gem thing. I thought you'd like it. If you were doing your housework on a hot day and wanted a soft drink, like root beer, why, all you would have to do is to put the thingamajig in it, and, presto, you'd have a soft drink. I thought you'd like it, and I bought it because I was walking on Van Buren Street and thinking of bringing you home a surprise. I was. I saw it in a drugstore window last week, and I was meaning to get it, but I kept forgetting, so this morning I tied a piece of string on my finger to make myself remember it. . . . And I did remember it."

"Your beans are getting cold," she said curtly.

He went on eating.

"If you don't want it, Peg, I'll bring it back in the morning."

"We'll keep it," she said. Then she laughed in a rather forced manner. "And you tied a piece of string around your finger to remember it?"

"Well, anybody can forget. I have so much to re- member on the job, and what difference does it make if I do tie a string around my finger as long as it turns the trick for me?"

"I'm going to get you a ball of twine, and I'm go- ing to give you a little piece of it every day to help you remember."

"Remember what?"

"So many things. For one thing, you didn't aim straight and I had to scrub up the bathroom floor again."

Walt gazed off in embarrassment.

"I'm sorry, Peg," he said humbly.

"Go on, Walt, dear, eat your beans before they get cold," she went on calmly.

Walt went on eating.

I I

"It won't work, I know it won't," Peg said im- patiently.

"Yes, it will. I read the booklet about it, and it's easy to work."

"Even if it does work, it won't work for you."

"Why won't it work for me?" Walt asked, stand- ing by the table and looking down at Peg.

"Don't ask me. I just know it won't. You never fixed anything right in the house."

"But I always did. And if we had our own home, you'd see how much I could do."

"You know, Walt dear, everything you do always comes out wrong. If you wash the dishes, I have to do them over again. The last time you washed the windows, I had to hire a man to do the job all over, they were so smudged."

"But, Peg, they weren't," Walt said sincerely. He remembered, yes, he remembered very clearly, that he'd done a good job with the windows.

"Go on, now, get your Little Gem whipped cream or whatever it is."

"I'll pour the coffee first and squirt it right in, and we'll have whipped cream floating on top of the coffee."

Walt went to the kitchen and returned with two cups of coffee, which he set on the table, one in front of Peg and one before his own place, opposite hers. Then he went back to the kitchen again to get the syphon. It was a cylindrical-shaped, chromium-finished bottle with a handle to be pressed.

"All I did was to pour the cream into the syphon, screw in the Gold Seal Whiplash, they call it—it's like a bullet—and let it cool in the icebox. Now watch and see—and, presto, I'll show you how practical and handy this thingamagig is."

Peg sighed in boredom.

Walt went to her and, leaning over, held the mouth of the syphon above her coffee cup.

"Now, don't make a splash and shoot it out like a stream," she said sharply.

"Don't worry, Peg . . ."

Walt became confused, hesitated for a moment, and then pressed the handle. The whipped cream shot out. A quick look of disgust and abhorrence crossed Peg's face. The cream and coffee were splashed on her clothes, on her face, on the table, and even on the wall.

"I told you not to do it!" she screamed.

Walt stood back, completely confused and awkwardly holding the syphon.

"It was an accident. I'll clean it up. I guess I pressed too hard or something."

"You'll clean it up?" she asked, glaring at him.

"It isn't serious, Peg. It's just a little mess. It was an accident."

"Just a little mess. Look at the wall. You've ruined my dress. The coffee was hot and burned my face. Just a little mess? For years, Walt Callahan, you've been making just a little mess for me."

"Here, I'll get a rag and clean it up," he said, turning to hurry into the kitchen.

The kitchen was spotlessly clean. He stood in the center of the room, holding the syphon and not knowing what to do.

"What's the matter with you? You're as clumsy as a horse," Peg shouted after him.

He didn't remember what he wanted. Then he realized he was looking for a rag. He was afraid he wouldn't find it. Then he saw one on the side of the sink. He picked it up, started back to the dining room, turned around, stopped, and became almost panicky. He looked at the syphon, which he was still holding.

"Well, you can explain to the landlord why his walls are stained, I won't!" Peg announced loudly.

He quickly set down the syphon on the kitchen table and returned to the dining room.

"It won't stain the walls, Peg."

Peg was wiping her face with a handkerchief. She grabbed the rag out of his hand and snapped:

"Let me do it. I'm always cleaning up after you anyway."

She energetically wiped the few splotches of cream and coffee from the wall. They left a stain.

"Mess and dirt and mess and dirt. I never saw a man who was as messy as you. All I do is work for you from morning to night, and there's no end to it."

She wiped the table, picked up her coffee cup, and went to the kitchen.

Walt stood for a moment, ungainly, his long arms hanging at his sides. He shook his head sadly from side to side. Then he went to the kitchen and said, "I'm sorry, Peg."

"Now the coffee's cold. I'll have to heat it again, and it will be too strong. Well, if you keep on drinking strong coffee, you'll get ulcers, and then I suppose they'll say I did it. No matter what I do, there's no end to it. I suppose I might as well give up."

"Peg, I only shot it too hard and got a little coffee and whipped cream on the wall and the table."

"And what about me?" she snapped, turning around and glaring at him again.

"I didn't hurt you," he said.

"You could have scalded me. You could have squirted coffee in my eye and blinded me."

"But I didn't, Peg, and I didn't mean to—"

"Go get your coffee cup, and I'll fix things. You should have let me do it in the first place."

Walt brought in the coffee cup. Then he returned to the dining room and sat down, waiting, again shaking his head from side to side.

—But it was only a little accident, he explained to himself.

Peg came in carrying two cups of coffee with whipped cream floating on top.

"See, Peg, it does work. It makes whipped cream out of just ordinary cream. And you can make ice cream with it, too," Walt said eagerly.

Peg sat down opposite him and drank her coffee in silence.

I I I

Walt sat comfortably slouched in his chair, soothed by the music from the radio. There was a soft, sleepy expression on his face. But he wished Peg would come in and listen to the music with him. Maybe now and then he'd say something to her, or she'd talk, and maybe they would talk about the past when they were young and about things they'd done together, the places they'd gone, the people they'd known, and of the days when their kids had been young. Peg was resting quietly now, but she made him kind of nervous, because she seemed sore, and if he went out to the bedroom and tried to talk to her, she might bite his head off or something. She was in one of those silent moods of hers that gave him the jitters. She'd complained about how tired she was, but she'd said it in a way that almost made him think it was his fault. Hell, he'd worked harder than she had today. She hadn't had much house cleaning to do, and it didn't take much time to cook frankfurters and heat a can of baked beans, did it? And it had been rugged all day down at the Depot. Tuttle, the Depot foreman, had hardly given him a minute's peace. But, hell, he didn't want to think of things like that now. He just wanted to sit here in peace.

The music. It was soft, the kind of music that used to make him feel sad and want to fall in love when he was young. Hearing it now made him feel lonely. Yes, he was lonely. Growing old, knowing you were spending the last years of your life with your wife should make you and her feel close together. You should be able to understand each other almost without having to say anything. You should feel close, the two of you remembering many happy days together and knowing you had each other. That was the way it should be, because that way would make living less lonely, especially in the evenings, like now, because, well . . . because at night you were just fagged out. And the night made you think how the sun had gone down for you on still another day while you were on the other side of the hill, the side of the hill that goes down, down. And he'd like to think of himself and Peg going down the hill together, hand in hand. He guessed that most men felt like this when they started getting old. And he could remember how, time and again, he used to imagine what it would be like when he and Peg began to get old, and the kids would be raised and married and have kids of their own. And now, think of it, the time had come, and he and Peg were old, an old couple. He used to imagine himself sitting in his chair of a night, just as he was doing at this very minute. And he'd seen himself and Peg talking and remembering, looking back on things and sometimes chuckling and laughing together, and having a bond of closeness as they would look back and talk about their good days together, and he'd imagined that these nights, as he'd dreamed of them, would be the best part of life and would give him feelings of being warm and contented inside. But, no, it wasn't turning out this way, not tonight, and not on most other nights either, because if it wasn't one thing that riled Peg it was another. And, come to think of it, he and Peg had lots they could remember and talk about, like courtship, and the plans they used to make, and dances and walks in the moonlight. God, in those days Peg had been as beautiful as "That Old Sweetheart of Mine." And then there was that time when both the kids had had pneumonia, and the way it had hit him just as if Jack Dempsey had socked him right flush in the solar plexus. He'd been no good then, and he remembered going to work on those cold winter mornings like a man in a daze. She'd been so wonderful, up night and day with the kids, taking better care of them than a trained nurse could have, and that was when she'd been most beautiful. That was when the going had been rough, and they'd pulled through. Now it ought to be easy, and they ought to enjoy the coming on of old age. Why didn't they?

Hell, what was he doing to cause all these rows and fights?

Walt sighed.

He remembered, too, how he used to think that when he got old he'd have Peg by his side if he got sick, and that she'd take care of him and he wouldn't feel he was alone. Right now, he felt pretty much alone.

God, yes, Peg had been a beautiful girl, and he'd loved her.

He sighed again. The music. It brought back all sorts of memories and feelings, and it made him think of things he'd wanted to have and never did have. That's why the music seemed so sad to him tonight, because when he had been young, music and songs like this had spelled out happiness to him.

Gee, he wished they'd play *When You and I Were Young, Maggie*.

I V

Lying in bed in the darkness, Peg thought of how, even without reading the booklet of instructions or ever having seen the syphon before, she had used it better than Walt. She couldn't understand how he had ever been a teamster and driven a team of horses. He was so clumsy and couldn't be relied on. How awkward and crude he'd been making love to her. God Almighty, could she ever forget him, fumbling at his fly and in long underwear or those B.V.D's men used to wear?

She giggled.

She remembered him before his hair was gray, tall and thin and strong, but, God, how clumsy he used to be, and he'd often made her feel almost sick. She had shuddered, and she had once said something to him about a horse—told him that he got into bed like a horse, or something like that.

Now she could see that during their whole life together he'd never understood her. If he understood her, he wouldn't be sitting in the parlor like a log, paying no attention to her when she was nervous and blue. If he had just the slightest understanding of her, he'd come to her now. But, no, he sat in the parlor with his newspaper and the radio, and with that sly, cunning look on his face. She might just as well be living alone as with him. How could she be more unhappy without him? How? Why, it was just the same as living alone, except that she had to wait on him hand and foot.

She'd never really wanted to marry him. God, why had she? He'd done it, done it to her. That night she'd cooked dinner for him when her mother and father had gone out.

The scene came back to her. Her mother, fat and gray-haired, telling her:

—The way to a man's heart is through his stomach.

Mother had wanted to get rid of her. Since her sixteenth birthday, and even before then, her mother had tried to get rid of her, to marry her off. And that night when she'd cooked dinner for Walt, Mother had known. Mother had just about told her to do it. That look in Mother's eyes. Her mother had done this to her. God, she hated to think this way of the dead, but it was true, it was, it was so. Could she ever forget that look in her mother's eyes that night? Her mother, with that look, had told her to go to bed with Walt. Her mother might just as well have made a whore of her.

That night at dinner, she should have seen him for what he was. She could almost see him now, sitting like a log, just as he was now in the parlor, and stuffing himself. He hadn't really appreciated her then. He'd broken a plate when he'd helped her wash the dishes. And then, sitting in the parlor with her. She couldn't think of that now. The pain, the humiliation of it. What a fool, what an innocent young fool she'd been.

Oh, God, why had it all happened to her? And now it was too late. Here she was with her ruined life. Oh, why had her life been wasted this way? How could she go on? Go on, for what? Go on until he got weak, and she had to nurse him like a cripple, wash him and bathe him and give him a bedpan the way her grandmother used to for her lazy old grandfather?

She'd only been a girl when her grandfather had died, but her mother had always talked of it and complained about how her grandmother had had to wait on the lazy old man hand and foot. Mother of God, was this to be her fate?

V

A Long, Long Trail A-Winding. . . . Even though this song made him sadder, he liked to hear it played over and over and over again.

Listening attentively, it was almost as if he weren't here in this room at all but somewhere else, by himself. He was so sad that he was almost happy in his sadness . . . *the Land of my Dreams* . . . He was in the land of his dreams, land of dreams in his own mind . . . and . . . *marching Down that long, long Trail* . . . that's what he'd wanted, to march down the long, long trail of life with Peg and to know some of the happiness promised in the song.

Yes, the things he'd wanted in life and hadn't gotten were there in the song. And it made him think of Peg, too, when she'd been a young girl. Sometimes he used to think of her as his Irish rose. He'd like to hear that song, too, *My Wild Irish Rose.* That's what he used to call her . . . his wild Irish rose. And that line in the song, *take the bloom from my wild Irish rose . . . a long, long night awaiting until.* . . . Peg had been a beautiful girl, all right. . . . Good God, what had happened, and why did people change so much?

The song ended. Walt slumped in his chair. The radio announcer was selling something. He didn't listen. He was lost in his own thoughts. He wanted to remember, to think of Peg when she had been his wild Irish rose. God, how proud he'd been of her and how he'd thought he wasn't good enough for her or worthy of her, and how he was even lousy to want to take her innocence. He remembered how he'd gone to her house for supper. That was years ago, when he'd just about come to believe he'd lost her, and then she'd invited him to dinner. All day on the wagon he'd looked forward to the time when he'd see her, and he'd been afraid, afraid of what he'd say and do and of what she'd say, and afraid that she'd turn him down and think him a fool.

That had been in June, a long time ago, back at the beginning of that long, long winding trail of his. He'd been young and strong then, and on that day he'd wrestled boxes, feeling almost as if he were an iron man. And he'd imagined Peg watching him tossing boxes over the tail gate of the Continental Express wagon and admiring him for his strength. And, singing to himself, he'd talked to Nellie, his horse, as he'd driven her clopping along Canal Street. He'd thought that Peg, if she would only have him, would give him an incentive, something to work for. God, he'd thought many things on that day. And, just think, it had been years ago. Walt sighed again.

V I

Walt grew nervous when Peg came into the parlor and sat on the big couch opposite his chair by the radio. He glanced guiltily at her and then looked off at a picture on the wall. It was a reproduction of an oil painting called "Indiana Sunset" which he'd won years ago in a church raffle. He thought it was very pretty, but he hadn't really noticed it for years.

"I was tired," Peg said in a normal, friendly tone of voice, which surprised him.

"I was listening to the radio."

She didn't answer. What should he say now? Maybe she didn't want the radio on, but a man had to do something at home of an evening, especially when he couldn't talk to his wife for fear of having her jump down his throat.

"Don't you want to listen to the radio, Peg? They've been playing old-time songs."

She didn't answer him.

"Peg," he blurted out, "I'm sorry I was a little bit careless with that syphon. I didn't mean anything by it. I guess I just pressed too hard and it came out too fast. But it did make good whipped cream, didn't it, and it wasn't such a bad—"

"You always were careless," she interrupted, "and you never did give me enough consideration."

"Peg, I'm sorry, I never meant any—"

"It's about time you said you were sorry. I was in there for hours and I had to come in here before you'd say it."

Hours? That was an exaggeration. But, then, there was no use in correcting her on this. It would only make her sore.

"But, Peg, I thought you were sleeping, and I didn't want to disturb you."

"How could I sleep with the radio going?"

"It wasn't on loud—was it?"

"If it wasn't blasting, it was nearly blasting."

"I'm sorry, Peg. If you'd only called me, I'd have turned the dial and made it softer. Here, I'll do it now."

"Don't bother," she said as he started to rise from his chair.

He sank back in the chair.

"Peg, I'll try, and let's forget it."

He waited anxiously for her answer, hoping she'd say something to show she'd gotten over being angry.

"Just be careful and don't act like a horse any more or treat our home here like a stable, and we won't have any trouble."

"I'll try, Peg."

She smiled at him.

"Come on, Peg," he said, rising, "slip me a kiss."

She rose slowly and let him kiss her. He hugged her tightly and then looked at her shyly and askingly.

He could do it tonight. He could. He knew he could.

He took her by the hand, but as he started to lead her out of the parlor, the telephone rang. Peg rushed to answer it.

V I I

"Yes, Dorothy, your father's well. Yes, the old man's as healthy as a horse," Peg said on the telephone, laughing.

She was good-humored now, and Walt felt better, only he wished the phone call hadn't come just at this minute. He sat on the bed in their room, waiting. He was uneasy and felt as if he'd done something wrong. But, hell, she was his wife. Still, look at their ages. At their ages, they should be done with it, shouldn't they? But, God, to think that at his age he wasn't all done below the belt, but now and then could still do it, that made a man a little proud, didn't it? What would Dorothy think if she knew that her phone call had come just when? She knew what men were like now. She loved Joe Zarilla, and they were happy. He loved his daughter; she was a good girl.

"And he's all thumbs, dear," Peg was saying, laughing lightly. "Yes, he brought home some new gadget to make whipped cream and . . ." Peg laughed again . . . "and he squirted it all over the wall and all over me instead of in the coffee."

Hell, it hadn't been that bad.

"No, your father, the old dear, he's not like Joe. Of course, he's an old dear, but around the house here—I have to do everything. I'm never done picking up after him. You wouldn't believe your eyes if you saw how much work one man can cause. Darling, you just can't know how clumsy he is. But, he's an old dear anyway."

Walt thought that Peg wasn't fair in what she was saying. But then, what the hell, since Peg was saying it all in a good-humored way, it wasn't so bad. Come to think of it, years ago, he used to be pleased and flattered when she talked about him like this.

He yawned. Now he was getting sleepy. And he felt relieved. He guessed that he hadn't really wanted to, and he was kind of glad he wouldn't have to. Hell, two weeks ago after it he'd felt . . . well . . . he'd felt pretty rotten and as if he shouldn't have done it. He'd sometimes felt that way, or more or less the same way, the few times with Peg before they were married. God, he wondered how other men felt about it.

"Dorothy, you don't know your father the way I do," Peg went on.

Sometimes he thought that growing old had its advantages because you didn't always like having that fever and desire as much as you pretended you did, and sometimes it left you feeling worse than if you had a hangover. If only growing old could be peaceful. Yet when he sometimes thought of Peg in the past, it hurt. But many things in your life hurt; yes, they hurt more if you thought too much about them.

Peg was laughing at him again. He wished she wouldn't do that with Dorothy, but then he guessed that Dorothy understood him. How long would Peg talk? He'd called in that he wanted to speak to Dorothy, too, but Peg was going on and on, making fun of him. Hell, goddamn it, he wasn't the loogin and clumsy ox she made him out to be. But maybe it was because he hadn't been . . . well, man enough with her that it turned out this way. Still, there had been times when he had, and there had been other times when he'd want her so badly and she'd keep him waiting, and then she'd start a fight with him and nag him just when he was getting in the saddle, and even when he was in the saddle. He guessed that he really didn't know what to think. He wasn't educated, and he hadn't read the books, and he didn't know lots of things, but, damn it, hadn't he tried and done the best he could? He just didn't know what to think.

Walt became nervous and impatient and got up and moved about. He wanted to talk to his daughter Dorothy. But Peg was still talking and laughing at him.

V I I I

When he finally got to the telephone, Walt was happy to hear Dorothy's voice.

"How are the kids?" he asked. Peg hadn't asked about their grandchildren.

"Oh, Father, they're wonderful. And they're always talking about you. They love to see you."

Walt choked up. It made him grateful. And Dorothy's voice, it was so girlish.

"I'll have to come over some Sunday soon."

"Yes, we want you to, Father. You know you're always welcome, and how much Joe likes to see you, too."

"Joe's a fine fellow, Dorothy."

He wanted to call her Lovely, because that was what he'd called her when she'd been a baby and a little girl, but he couldn't quite get himself to.

Peg was listening, so he had to be careful of what he was saying, because sometimes she criticized him for what he said to the kids on the phone, and then there was a row.

33

"Is Mother giving it to you?" Dorothy asked him with an understanding and affectionate little laugh.

"Well . . . " he didn't know what to say.

"Father, darling, don't let it get you. Don't worry. You know how she is, and she doesn't mean it. She's just that way. You know Mother, Daddy."

"Yes, of course I do. And you're well?"

"Yes, knock on wood."

Now Peg was pacing back and forth near the phone, and this distracted him and made it even harder for him to talk to Dorothy.

"Well, we'll be coming over soon."

"Yes, Father, please do."

"And Joe's okay?"

"He's bowling tonight. He's in some tournament and he's got a new ball. He said he was going to bowl a two-hundred game, but I kidded him and told him he didn't have the stuff in him."

"What did he say?"

"Oh, he laughed. You know Joe, Daddy."

"Yes, he's okay by me, Dorothy."

A pause. Peg pacing up and down. He wanted to talk longer, but his mind went blank.

"Well, I'll see you soon."

"Do, Daddy, please."

"I will."

"Good-by."

"Good-by, Daddy darling, and here's a kiss."

She blew him a kiss over the phone.

"Good-by . . . " he said.

He heard the click as Dorothy hung up. He sat with the receiver to his ear, bewildered and choked up with gratitude. His daughter loved and respected him.

He put the receiver back, got up, and looked at Peg, embarrassed. He couldn't do anything now.

"I think I'll have a glass of beer and turn in, dear," he said quickly because of his embarrassment.

"I'll get it for you. You'll spill it if you get it yourself."

She hurried to the kitchen to get his beer, and he went slowly to the dining-room table. Hell, he knew how to pour a glass of beer without spilling it. But he'd better let well enough alone and drink the beer in quiet, and then he'd hit the hay.

I X

Walt remembered how, when he'd been in his twenties and even his thirties, he'd wake up fresh and clear-eyed and feeling his oats. He hadn't really appreciated how strong and healthy he'd been. . . . Back in his days on the wagon, he'd tossed plenty of boxes and crates around and wrestled many a barrel. And he'd never gotten a rupture, either. He'd just taken his strength for granted. And in those days, the minute he woke up he'd be wide awake. Hell, he sure wasn't the man he used to be. Now on most mornings he woke up gloomy, sometimes feeling aches and pains, just as he did this morning, and he even wondered how he could get through the day. Of course, he knew he could face the day, and that after his coffee he'd begin to wake up, and once he got out and into the air, he'd feel pretty good. But he never used to wake up blue and in the dumps, as he did these days, morning after morning. And then, washing and shaving and fixing his own breakfast—the worst of it was eating alone. He guessed he really couldn't ask Peg to get up at five-thirty or six, only he wished she would of her own free will. She could go back to sleep after he left, couldn't she? But if he asked her, she'd raise the roof, and if he got sore and put his foot down and tried to make her, then she might do it and nag him for it, so he guessed it was better to be lonely in peace than to have company without peace. It made him think of that old joke about single blessedness or double wretchedness. Damn it, it got you to think of how once he'd been so young and strong, and Peg so beautiful, and to remember how so many people had talked about what a fine young couple they were. And now—but what was the use of thinking this way?

He began to drink his second cup of coffee and thought of how he had been getting up early and going to work for years and years. Yes, he'd gone on all these years, putting his shoulder to the wheel, and he was still doing it. He'd gone out in the darkness on many a cold morning, and it had been mighty damn freezing on some of those days when he'd driven a wagon. Just to remember them almost made him feel cold and imagine it was winter instead of spring. God, he didn't know how he'd stood some of those days on the wagon, strong as he'd been. And he remembered how he used to think he wasn't wrestling freight and fighting cold only for himself, but for Peg and his kids. Now, well, it was for Peg and himself, and, well, he wished she were different. These days he kept coming back to the same thoughts more and more. And he kept thinking of other days, of what used to be, and of the way he used to imagine it might all turn out. But there had been a time when he used to come home to Peg proud, and see her such a pretty, such a beautiful young mother.

He took another sip of coffee. Yes, it had been a long, long time since he'd driven an express wagon. He knew it was foolish to wish himself back on the wagons and starting out all over again, but he did wish it. He wished he were young right now, only if he was young he'd be on a big truck or a tractor— that is, if he'd be an expressman. Hell, he couldn't be anything else but an expressman, because that was all he knew.

He took another sip of coffee.

Think of how the express business had changed, and how the horse, man's best friend, was gone, and sometimes he almost thought he was just like an old horse. He'd had his day. Only, had it been as good a day as it might have been?

And then, God, he remembered how proud he'd

been the night during the First World War, when he'd come home and told Peg that he'd been made Wagon Dispatcher and would get one hundred and seventy-five dollars a month. Come to think of it, that had been a damned good salary back in those days. Peg had taken the news mighty casual, as if she didn't particularly care. They'd even had a big fight that night. He couldn't recollect now just what had caused the fight and why they'd had to have a fight on a night when they should have been celebrating, but he did remember how he'd gone to bed feeling damned lousy, as lousy as he'd felt last night. But then, on that night Peg had crawled into bed and kissed him and said she was sorry, and he'd told her how sorry he was, and they'd agreed they would never fight again. It had been good that night, so good that, damn it, he'd worshiped her!

He took another sip of coffee, lit a cigarette, and sadly gazed at the white ceiling.

Suddenly he thought of Patsy McLaughlin. Patsy had made him a Dispatcher. Patsy was dead. He'd always called him Patsy. You couldn't call Mr. Cartwright, who now had Patsy's old job, by his first name. But, then, Patsy had been an old-timer, coming up from the wagons himself. He still found it hard to believe that Patsy was dead. It didn't seem true that he'd be going to work today and not expect Patsy to be coming into the Depot in his Ford coupé. And think of the other old-timers who were gone, too. Jim O'Neill had passed away many years ago.

He'd been a good man. One of his kids, who used to work in the Call Department, had become a famous writer. Well, more power to the kid. More power to anyone who made something out of themselves. And McGinty, they used to call him the Gashouse. What a bull Mac had been. Mac was gone, too. And Mike Mulrooney and Wade Norris and Willie Bryan; they'd always called Willie Father Bryan. They were all gone now. He'd attended the wakes of every one of them; why, he'd even been one of Willie Bryan's pallbearers. And Billie O'Brien, he was gone, too. Billie's going last year had been heartbreaking. Poor fellow, having to go on a pension before his time because of a heart attack, a coronary. And then passing away four months after his retirement.

God, how many old-timers would be left when his time came?

God Almighty, he would die one day, and it wouldn't be too many years away. A man of his age couldn't count on living many more years, could he? He was gripped with fear. He'd have to go, and he didn't want to, and suppose he had to suffer terrible pains before he went? He'd hate to be bedridden, moaning in agony, and maybe lying there, and thinking about his life, thinking about what he'd never got and of his dreams that had never come true. And would Peg nag even when he would be on his deathbed and not even let him die in peace? But suppose she went first?

He saw himself alone in this little apartment, get-

39

ting up in the morning, just as he did this morning, cooking breakfast, going to work, and then, after his day's work was done, feeling free, able to do anything he wanted to. But what would it mean for a man of his age to be free? No, if that happened, he'd go live with Dorothy or with his son Jack, if either of them would have him.

Wasn't it awful to think this way of Peg dying? He felt ashamed of having such thoughts. A man shouldn't think this way. Maybe it was even a sin. And a man should keep trying to make the best of things. Only . . .

Now it was time to go to work. He picked up his dishes, took them to the sink and washed them, leaving them in the rack to dry. Then he tiptoed out of the kitchen and into the bedroom, resolving to be as quiet as possible so as not to wake Peg.

X

"You don't have to come in here like a bull in a china shop," Peg accused him angrily from the bed.

"I was very quiet, Peg," Walt answered, hurt, as he turned from the closet door with his suit coat in his hand.

"Quiet? As quiet as a herd of elephants."

"I'm sorry, Peg, I tried to be very quiet."

"You wake me up every morning. You don't care

about anyone but yourself, tramping and stamping through the house, banging doors and drawers. How can I go on if you don't let me sleep?"

"I'm sorry, Peg."

"You're sorry? A fat lot of good that does me."

"But I didn't mean, Peg . . . I didn't bang no drawers this morning. I didn't touch them."

"Well, you woke me up yesterday morning slamming drawers."

"But, Peg, you were asleep yesterday morning when I left for work."

"No, I wasn't. Are you going to stand there, Walt Callahan, and lie to my face out of the whole cloth?"

"I'm not lying, Peg."

"I'd be ashamed of myself if I lied the way you do, Walt Callahan."

"Peg, I'm sorry—and I got to go to work now if I ain't gonna be late."

"You don't have to make as much noise as a house-wrecking company when you go to work."

Walt checked himself as he was about to answer her. If he got into an argument now, he'd be late.

"Peg, I'm sorry. Here, kiss me good-by and try and get back to sleep and get some rest," he said, going over to the bed.

"How can I sleep after you woke me up?"

"Well, try, Peg, dear."

He bent down to kiss her. She raised her cheek to him, but her face was coldly expressionless.

"Good-by and have a good, easy, restful day, Peg," he said as he turned to walk softly out of the bedroom.

"Yes, have an *easy* day," she mumbled to herself.

X I

It was going to be another swell day, Walt thought, walking along to the streetcar. But on mornings like this the June sunshine kind of hurt. It made him remember early mornings in June back in the days when he was on the wagon and had first met Peggy. He'd felt so happy then, walking along in the early-morning sunshine, smelling the early morning—why, he used to feel as if the world was . . . well . . . was full of sap, and the world and life were mighty good, and just honey. And Peg, she seemed to be like everything that was good in the world and like the morning, like a beautiful morning. Yes, a swell morning like this just took all the starch out of him now.

He walked along at a slow, even, treadlike pace.

He remembered Peg this morning, nagging him about making noise, when, hell, he'd been quiet. It was just like so many other things about her. He just never knew when he was going to put his foot in it with her and when she was going to blame him for something out of a clear sky, and then, well, when she talked like she did to him this morning, she sent him to work down in the mouth and sunk.

At sixty-three, damn it, a man ought to feel contented, because he was going to be called soon, and at least you wanted to feel at peace as you came close to the call. God, back in those first days of their marriage, Peg used to hug and kiss him at the door and tell him not to get hurt and to come straight home from work because she'd be waiting for him, and sometimes in the morning they'd do it, and he'd go to work grinning and just thinking, goddamn it, he felt good, and he'd think of her and of her dark eyes, and of the sun and the morning, and she had been June to him, June sunshine.

And, think of it, in seven years, he'd be seventy and retiring.

What would it be like then?

He walked on. Others were walking along, past the two- and three-story stone and brick buildings, going to work like him, and he wondered what their lives were like.

X I I

She didn't have the energy to get up. The morning must be passing, but she didn't care, she didn't want to stir out of bed.

When she'd been a little girl, she used to feel like this and would want to stay in bed where it was warm and where she could dream and not be afraid of anything. Because as long as she stayed in bed, quiet as a mouse, she felt that nothing could happen to her. She could remember herself lying in bed as long as she could, scarcely stirring. And how she used to dream and dream, imagining all sorts of things happening to her, sometimes pretending she was a boy and sometimes dreaming she was a bird. She used to love to think she was a bird and able to fly, to fly away, away far away from her mother and father.

She suddenly became afraid, but she didn't know what she was afraid of. She gazed about the dark room and then at the dim morning light in the hall outside the bedroom door. It seemed as if just beyond the bed there were danger lurking in wait for her.

Oh, she was unhappy, an unhappy woman. She had always been unhappy, always. Even as a child she'd been unhappy. And why should she have gotten out of bed then when her mother nagged her to? Why? To be abused and spat upon and to be told that she was no good on earth? Oh, her mother had never been good to her—no one in this world had ever been good to her. All her life she had only wanted someone to be good to her. That was all she wanted. Was it too much to ask from life? Was it?

Walt was a cold man, and no, never, never had he been good and really kind to her. She had given herself to him before marriage because, fool that she was, she'd believed that if she gave him her all, he'd be good to her. And now what was there to dream of? Oh, if she could only be a bird and fly away, fly away from it all?

She would still shudder, when she remembered the way her mother used to say to her:

—You're a girl.

She must have been seven when her mother said to her:

—Peg, you'll never have a peg.

And that time her father beat her mother, it was like a nightmare.

Her father, drunk and cursing, chasing her mother around the dining-room table, cursing, oh, he had cursed so. And her mother, screaming and begging him not to hit her, but taunting him, too, and threatening him with a butcher knife. And she in the corner, wishing there were some hole she could crawl into, wishing she were a mouse, able to get into a crack in the wall.

Ugh!

He beat her mother, and she fell on the floor and sobbed, and then her father came toward her, and she ran around the table, too frightened to cry or scream, and she ran because she didn't want him to touch her, and he caught her, and she'd been so afraid, and he'd held her on his lap and squeezed her and tickled her, and his breath had been so vile, smelling of beer. It all burned in her memory. And she remembered how she only wanted to get away, to bed, anywhere, and she hadn't wanted to get up and go to school the next morning, and she had lain in bed thinking she was a bird.

She began to move nervously in bed, and then she

jumped up and threw her kimono on. Trembling, she searched the apartment as though she were looking for someone or something, and then she went out to the kitchen and turned on the gas under the coffee pot.

Yes, if she could only be a bird and fly away.

X I I I

Stretched out on the bed, Walt sighed with pleasure. It was peaceful at home, and he could lie here and not have to do anything until supper was ready. Peg was more herself, and things were just the way he wanted them. And think of it, he had come home worried and just about as down in the dumps as a man could get, expecting Peg to be ready to fly off the handle, but she hadn't, and she'd told him that she'd cleaned the house today and was cooking him a specially good supper, and she'd been so friendly, like her old self, she had been just like the Peg he wanted her to be. And she'd asked him about work today and said he must be tired and why didn't he take a nap? He'd asked her if there was anything he could do, and she'd said no, no, there wasn't, he should just take a nap and refresh himself because he worked hard and was the breadwinner.

He sighed again.

Peg was just nervous, that was all, and these spats and quarrels were not about anything important, and, my God, they had passed their thirty-ninth wedding anniversary, and when a man and woman were married almost forty years, these little spats had to be seen for what they were.

Yes, Peg was just nervous, that was it, and maybe he didn't do things the best way to suit her, and he'd watch his step more so he could please her on little things. Hell, at the Depot, he would sometimes want to blow his top if things didn't suit him, and today he'd come near to doing it with Willie Collins, the poor, pathetic loogin. Hell, yes, just as he was Dispatcher at the Depot, let Peg be Dispatcher at home here. If satisfying Peg would make things more peaceful and make her less nervous, then he'd make a real try.

Walt let out a big, comforting yawn.

There were good experiences in his life with Peg—the kids, grandchildren, memories. And maybe sometimes you foolishly let the good memories get washed out of your mind. You shouldn't let that happen. He'd have to keep this in mind when he got to brooding and stewing, so as not to let this happen again.

He could hear Peg in the kitchen. She was cooking for him. She did things for him, and she'd done them for over thirty-nine years, hadn't she? And hadn't he taken her when she was innocent and been the only man she'd ever known? After it happened in her parlor that first time, she'd cried because he'd hurt her, and she'd cried in pain, too. But then, later, there'd been times when she'd been so passionate that it had almost frightened him. Gosh, he guessed a man just couldn't understand a woman.

And their honeymoon. It was kind of vague in his mind, those two weeks. But it had been good, wonderfully good. Golly, how he'd like to see Niagara Falls again, that cataract of water going over and making noises like thunder. It had frightened Peg. He could remember how he'd just stood there and looked and thought of how much power there was in that water, and it had sure been one beautiful sight to see.

He closed his eyes and tried to see Niagara Falls, just as if it might be a picture in his mind. But it was hard to bring it back clearly. And then himself and Peg, Peg, a beautiful black-haired, black-eyed bride in a white dress and a straw hat, his Maid of the Mist, standing at the rail, and the water splashing, and that thunder of the water, and the foam and the colors of the water down below, and he'd just looked and looked and thought of God, and he'd wanted to stay and just look at the falls, only Peg had seen enough and said she wanted to go, so they hadn't stayed there that extra day the way he'd wanted to. And New York and Atlantic City and the Atlantic Ocean and Washington, D.C. At times, though, they'd both felt a little lost, especially in Washington, D.C., looking at the Government buildings. But just think—how long ago that was. Why, Woodrow Wilson had been President. And, come to think of it,

F.D.R. had been Assistant Secretary of the Navy. And now they were both dead, our two greatest Presidents since Lincoln. And look at all that had happened in the world since their honeymoon. Why, for him that was the olden times now. And yet it didn't seem so very long ago that he and Peg were getting on the train in Washington and coming back here to start their life and build a home and be happy.

Yes, he and Peg had had their whole life together, and shouldn't that be more important than any little squabbles? But, damn it, he hadn't even begun to enjoy all the happiness he'd hoped for when they were riding back on that train from Washington. He guessed, though, that no man ever saw his dreams come true. Still, he was going to try to get some peace and contentment out of these last years of theirs. And he was going to try to begin right now.

Walt let out another big, contented yawn. He listened to the sounds Peg was making in the kitchen with a quiet feeling of pleasure.

X I V

"Peg, this is a mighty fine supper you cooked."

"It could be better."

"It doesn't have to be any better to satisfy me. You know how I am, Peg. I don't want much, and I don't expect too much so long as things go along smooth."

He was trying to tell her that he wouldn't complain

49

and that it should be easy for them to get along and live in peace, if they just put their minds to it.

"Well, it's about time you changed."

"Have I changed, Peg?" he asked in surprise.

"It's about time you did."

"But, Peg, I don't . . ."

Walt stopped. He didn't want to say anything to precipitate a row.

"Peg, let us both just get along with each other. I was thinking, lyin' down just now, of our honeymoon. Remember Niagara Falls, Peg? And Atlantic City and the ocean and Washington, D.C.?"

"Yes," she said curtly.

"We had a good honeymoon, didn't we, Peg?"

"I didn't want to stay long in Niagara Falls."

"We didn't. Remember, Peg, you wanted to leave, so we did?"

"All there was to see was water. You can go to the lake front here and look at Lake Michigan if you want to look at water."

"Peg, let's just take a ride on the streetcar tonight and go sit by the lake. Remember, we did that a couple of times years ago?"

"And come home all worn out? I'm tired. I worked hard today. I cleaned the whole apartment and cooked and did the shopping. I'm so tired I can hardly eat."

"Well, let's do it some one of these nights."

Peg didn't answer. They went on eating.

Then she said:

"You never brought home all that back pay."

Walt was startled. He didn't know what she was talking about.

"You can't answer me. And you have a guilty look, too," she said, speaking rapidly.

"But . . . but, Peg . . . why, there ain't been no back pay in over a year."

"I don't care, I don't ask you to bring me home your pay check like some wives, but you could be a man, an honest man, and not lie to me."

"But, Peggy, I don't know about no back pay."

He tried to remember if he might be wrong and was forgetting some possible back pay he might have gotten. And he felt nervous, too, as if he'd really done something wrong. He tried to assure himself that his conscience was clear.

"You have the boldness to say to my face that you didn't lie to me and deceive me about that back pay? And when you have such a guilty look in your eye, too?"

"I ain't deceived you about any back pay, honest, I haven't, Peg hon," he said. "And I don't know about any guilty look in my eyes."

"And you came home that time laughing about McGinty."

"But, hon, McGinty is dead. He's been dead for years now."

"I know what you've been doing and what you've been like all these years," she snapped at him.

"But what have I been doing and what am I like?"

"I should have known better, but I did think that some day you would get off the wagons and not go on acting like a teamster."

This hurt him. He was . . . well . . . a little bit proud that he had come up from the wagons, and there was nothing wrong with a man having once been a teamster, was there?

"It's the manure," she went on, speaking with contempt.

And this hurt, too, especially because of the resolution he'd made a little while ago when he was lying down before supper.

"But, Peggy, what did I do," he asked rather plaintively.

"You know what you've done to me," she said almost tragically.

"I wish I did."

"There, there, you admit it," she snapped.

"What did I admit?" he asked, now utterly bewildered.

"You asked me what you did to me."

"But what's that got to do with what you've been saying?"

Peg began to cry. He sat, helpless.

His appetite was gone. What could he say? What could he do? What had he done? What was this all about?

X V

Peg seemed calmer after she had her coffee, but she looked old and sad, like a woman with some great suffering in her life. He was still hurt and puzzled by her outburst, but he felt sorry, too, seeing her this way, so sad, and noticing that she looked old, with lines under her eyes and little wrinkles at the corners of her mouth, and the gray in her hair. She had once been his wild Irish rose.

"I'll do the dishes now," she said dully.

"Peg, let's leave the dishes and take in a movie. It'll make us both feel better, and then I'll do them when we come home."

"Yes, and let my kitchen swarm with cockroaches," she answered.

"But if you just stack the dishes up in the sink, how will that bring on a swarm of cockroaches?"

"Mrs. Zale downstairs is filthy, and I don't know how we've escaped cockroaches. If I wasn't so clean, we'd have them, too."

"Yes, I always say you're one of the neatest little housewives there is."

"Oh, no, I'm not. But I don't want my home to be like a stable."

"And you're a wonderful cook."

"You didn't eat much. Look at all the food you wasted."

"I really liked it, I did, only I . . . oh, come on, Peg, let's take in a movie at the corner."

"I have a headache."

"I'll get you some aspirin. Here, let me get you some aspirin and then let me do the dishes."

He ran to the bathroom and returned with aspirin. But she wouldn't take it.

"Peg, let me do the dishes."

"Yes, and leave grease on the plates so I'll be ill next time I use them."

"Well, if I do that, you tell me and I'll do them over."

"And you'll keep me in the kitchen like a slave."

He started to say something else but stopped. He forgot what he had just wanted to say to her. He stood with his long arms akimbo. Then he shrugged his shoulders and walked dejectedly into the parlor.

X V I

Walt was sitting in his chair. When Peg was like this, the way she'd been tonight, the nights were long, and he didn't know what to do with himself.

He got restless, and he couldn't keep his mind on his newspaper, and he couldn't even concentrate and listen if he turned on the radio. If he went to a movie by himself, then maybe she'd raise the roof. If she'd go to a movie with him, it would be good for her, an escape, but he just couldn't make up his mind to get up, go out into the kitchen where she was ironing, and try to convince her. And he felt that he had better not go to the show alone. But, hell, why did she have to be ironing at this hour? Didn't she have all day tomorrow? He just didn't get the logic or sense of how Peg did things.

The parlor was clean and neat. Peggy kept things clean, all right, but she wore herself out doing it. He appreciated it, but, then, he had worked all his life and supported her. She had never gone in want, nor had he beaten her up the way some fellows beat their wives. God, in what way was he unfair to her? But sometimes he felt as if he were. And night after night he was unhappy, just as he was now. Why did he have to come home from work to nights like this?

"Oh!" Peg exclaimed.

He looked up. But she was already on her way out of the room.

"Peggy?" he called.

There was no answer.

"Peggy?" he called more loudly.

She came back to the parlor.

"You don't have to scream at me," she yelled.

"I wasn't screaming."

"I'll ask Mrs. Condon next door if you weren't."

"But, Peggy, I didn't notice you come in and just called to ask if you wanted something or wanted me to do something for you?"

"If I did, I'd have to get down on my knees and plead with you."

"But, Peggy—" he began.

She interrupted, talking very rapidly.

"You shout around here the same way you do at the express Depot. You treat your own home as if it were a Depot. Can't you ever forget the Express Company and be—"

"But, Peggy, I wasn't thinking about the Express Company or work."

"Be a man and have a little refinement and gentleness."

Walt was too surprised to say a word or to know what he thought. He just wanted Peg to stop. If she would only be quiet and not fly off the handle this way and keep nagging him.

"Peggy . . ." he began.

He was going to ask her please to calm down and then to let them both forget this quarreling and bickering. But she walked out of the room again.

He slumped in the chair. Sometimes he felt like hitting her. Sometimes he kind of thought that what she really needed was a good punch in the nose or for him to grab her and put her across his knees and just paddle that behind of hers until it hurt. But he knew he wouldn't do it. No, a man couldn't hit a woman. God, he remembered that time when he was a kid, he must have been ten, and his mother and his old man were screaming at each other, and his old man hit his mother. He could still remember his mother just crumbling up and falling, and himself, with all of the Bejesus just frightened out of him, and for maybe a minute or two he'd even been afraid his father had killed his mother. It had made him just sick and so afraid, he'd shaken in a corner. And he'd hated his father for it, and after that he'd always had different feelings toward his mother and father. And he'd remembered this when he'd married Peg, and he'd vowed to himself never to hit her. Sore as he often got with Peg, he'd never hit her, and he was proud of himself for that. God, though, thinking now of his old man beating up his mother gave him a sad feeling of uselessness. They were both dead, may God have mercy on their souls. It was as if it didn't matter now what they'd done, or what it meant to him and his brothers and sisters. It was all long ago, and here he was at sixty-three remembering it. And how he'd been knocked for a loop, too, when his mother had died. He'd been sunk then, but he'd told himself that you had to be a man and face up to the sorrows of life, and this had helped him come out of the depression he'd felt.

He sighed. It was no use thinking of all kinds of sad things like that from a man's past.

The house was quiet. He hoped the storm was over now for the night. That sometimes happened. Peggy would blow up and act peculiar and suspicious and accuse him of all kinds of things, and then she'd calm down and you wouldn't think she was the same person she'd been only a little while ago.

He tried to read his paper, but he couldn't keep his mind on it.

He just wished Peg wouldn't nag him. God, he didn't know what he did that caused her to nag him so much. He'd always believed he was pretty much the same as other men. He didn't want to go on thinking about this. He became very uneasy. Sometimes he was afraid that maybe the reason Peg was so nervous and cranky was that he hadn't satisfied her. She acted toward him as if she had something against him and didn't respect him. Hell, he might as well be honest with himself and not kid himself. Yes, he guessed that this was pretty much true—Peggy didn't respect him.

But it hurt to admit this to himself. It did. It hurt. He was old, and he knew there were lines in his face. And he could feel his years in many ways. Sometimes he got tired. If he went at it too fast about the Depot, he'd puff. His legs got tired and achy if he was on them too much. And, God, when he looked at young dames, he felt it and knew it. Like last Sunday. He and Peg had taken a walk. He'd wanted to talk with her, just about little things and about when they were young. But he just hadn't been able to say anything. He had tried to, two or three times, but Peg had snapped at him, and then he hadn't been able to talk to her at all. She had put the damper on him.

And he'd thought that here were himself and Peg, alone, and their son and daughter were married. Yes, they were alone. They didn't see young Jack and Dorothy much, or their grandchildren, and they were alone, and they didn't even have much to say to each other unless it was to fight and squabble. Why, they were strangers to each other.

And he'd noticed the young girls. Peg had been a young girl once. And they had once strolled the way those young girls and fellows had last Sunday, some of them holding hands and in love so you could see it, acting and looking like nothing else in the world mattered but love.

And walking with Peg and thinking, his heart had suddenly gone out to her. He'd imagined she was thinking the same kind of thoughts he was thinking. Seeing so many pretty young girls on the streets, it must have hurt her.

Once he'd taken her hand and squeezed it and she'd squeezed back. He'd felt kind of close to her then, felt that they did have each other. But in a couple of minutes she'd snapped at him.

—You're beginning to walk like an old man, Walt.

—Well, Peggy, I'm not young any more, but I'm still not doing so bad. Lots of men are in worse condition than I am at my age.

—You're old. You look old. You act old. Why don't you buck up? I do. I don't just give up and say I'm an old woman the way you do.

—I'm not an old woman.

—You're sometimes like an old woman.

That hurt, too. He'd wondered was Peggy telling him the truth? For a few moments he'd wanted to crawl into something and hide his head.

And so they had just walked on in silence. But it

seemed to him that there were two kinds of silences. There was that being silent when you were feeling contented, and there was that being silent when you knew that if you weren't it would only mean arguing and misunderstanding and hurting each other. The kind of silence between them as they had walked had been no good.

And it had hurt all right to see the girls, all dressed up and pretty, with their hair done up, and their legs, the girls on the streets, and he couldn't help it, he just wished for what he knew he could never have again as long as he lived—a young girl. And then he got to thinking and wondering and asking himself questions. These young girls, God, they looked like the most beautiful things in the world. But did they have to end up like Peg? Because, yes, Peg had been as pretty as many of the girls he saw on the streets last Sunday. And when she was young and togged out in all her finery, why, old men must have looked at her in just the way he'd looked at the young girls last Sunday.

X V I I

"Well, dear, another day," Peg exclaimed calmly as she came into the parlor and sat down.

"Yes," Walt said cautiously, surprised at her change of mood.

"I finished the ironing."

"I'm glad."

"Do you want another cup of coffee, dear?"

"No, thanks, I might not sleep if I have too much."

"Yes, I don't think you should drink so much coffee."

"I think I'll start to cut down right away. I must have had six . . . no, eight cups of coffee today."

"That's too much. It isn't good for your health."

This remark scared him. Maybe this was the start of something, telling him he was old, that he was sick, or that maybe his heart wasn't good.

"I have to take better care of you, hon," she said.

"You do pretty good, Peg," he answered.

"I try. But I can't stop you from drinking too much coffee. Goodness knows I try, but you don't always listen to me."

"I will," he said.

He had wanted to add, "Mother," but somehow he stopped and didn't. He used to call her Mother, because of the kids and then because they had grandchildren. He'd always liked doing it, even though now and then he would have some kind of feeling, as if there was something in him, some voice or something inside him, that wanted to tell him he shouldn't call her Mother.

"You know, Peg, how it is down at the Depot. It gets noisy, and sometimes I get tired, and there are dull periods of the day, and . . . well, I guess I just got into the habit, so when I find myself feelin' tired and kind of dopey or groggy, why, I just tell my kid who writes sheets for me to run across the street and get a can of coffee. But I'll watch myself."

He looked down at the newspaper he had dropped on the floor by the side of his chair. He wanted to pick it up and read it, not because he was interested in the news but because this was one of those times with Peg when he didn't know what to say for fear of how she'd take it.

He didn't like to worry about himself, and he didn't like to think about his heart and about dying. At his age, a man could have a heart attack. Some did. He'd always been healthy, and there wasn't no need to worry, but you never could tell. Look at poor Billie O'Brien. Every day men his age were dropping off.

"You breathe fast, too. Sometimes I worry about you, Walt," Peg said.

"I don't breathe too fast, and I think my ticker's pretty good, considering my age," he said, speaking rather quickly.

"It isn't my fault. I've done my best. I've tried to see to it that you get rest, enough sleep, and the right food. It's not my fault."

Walt was sweating under the armpits.

"Maybe I ought to go to the doctor and get a checkup, have him listen to my ticker."

Peg made no comment.

She was gazing at the windows. There was a funny or a strange look in her eyes, as if she wasn't interested in him or in what he was saying but in something else, something that might be running through her head.

"Well, don't you want me to get it for you?"

"Get me what?" he asked, surprised by the question because for the moment he didn't recall her asking if he wanted her to get him anything.

"Coffee."

"No, I don't think I'd better take any more coffee tonight."

"Well, you asked me for it."

"I didn't—I didn't ask you, Peg. You asked me."

"You'd keep me running back and forth all night, serving you like a slave or working myself to the bone out there in the kitchen while you sit on your behind like the lord of the house, and I hardly get time to sit down for a few minutes' rest."

"But, Peggy . . ." he began, speaking slowly and in a low, dispirited voice.

He told himself that what she was saying was unfair.

"You don't have to treat me like a chauffeur. I'm not a teamster. I'm not a manure whaler the way you used to be when I first met you. And don't make faces at me. I've done nothing but slave for you and take care of you and wash your clothes. And do you realize how many times I've had to mop the bathroom floor because you can't hit the toilet bowl?"

Sometimes she said things to him that was like hitting below the belt. It was unfair. It was as if he were to throw up to her that she had the monthlies every month. He wanted to say it, but he couldn't just get the words out. He only thought it. He was too hurt to say anything.

"Every day, every time you go to the bathroom, you mess the floor."

"No, I don't. Maybe sometimes I'm a little care—"

"I can't remember a time since I married you that you didn't."

"Peggy," he pleaded.

She rose and paced back and forth in the room. Over the built-in mantel there was a mirror, and she paused to look at herself in it. He watched her, imagining that a drowning man must feel the way he did. He noticed she had changed the way she fixed her hair. She did it up in a wild kind of way; he couldn't describe it or tell himself what the difference was, except that she used to fix her hair simply, and now it was curled and puffed and different—well, just wild-looking.

She turned toward him.

"Why do you do this to me?"

"What am I doing? I haven't done anything to you, Peg."

"You know what you do to me," she accused, and then she laughed peculiarly.

"Peggy—let's not quarrel."

"I'm not quarreling. You're always quarreling and criticizing. It's you."

He was all mixed up.

"I wouldn't treat a dog, Walt Callahan, the way you've treated me."

"Oh, for Christ sake, Peg, dry up," he snapped, but not too angrily.

It was just that . . . that, well . . . that he didn't want to spend the night like this, being nagged.

"That's a fine way to talk to me. That's the kind of a man you are!"

"Well, Jesus Christ, a man doesn't want to be nagged day in and day out. Why don't you let up and not nag me so much?"

"You're the one who nags."

As he started to answer her, she turned her back on him, shook her hips, and walked about with dainty steps, laughing in a strange, somewhat high-pitched way.

"I'm not one who nags," she said in a gay falsetto. "I like to enjoy life and feel young. You're the old lady in this home, not me."

He watched her, nodding his head from side to side. God, was this Peg? Was this his wife? Was this the mother of his children? Was she the grandmother of his grandchildren? Was she the innocent young Peg he'd kissed and married? Was this his wild Irish rose?

She glared at him with burning eyes. He couldn't meet her gaze.

Peg was changed. She had put makeup on, and he hadn't remembered her having it on at supper. She looked really old now. And though he didn't like to admit it even to himself, she looked ugly. Her face was thin. Her complexion was sallow, and she looked unhealthy.

She let out a loud, wild laugh and screamed at him.

"You know, Tom, there's nothing you wouldn't stop at to hurt me. You know, Tom, what you want to do to me?"

He was so hurt, he didn't immediately take in the fact that she'd called him Tom instead of Walt. When he did realize this, it just mixed him up all the more. Then it came to him that Tom had been her father's name, old Tom Hennessey. He'd fallen off an express wagon, dead drunk, cracked his skull, and died.

"My name isn't Tom, it's Walt."

"Who said your name was Tom?" she asked angrily.

"Why, you just called me Tom."

"I didn't. You're lying. Walt Callahan, how will you ever dare face your God, lying about me as you do, and to my face. *Thou shalt not bear false witness against thy neighbor.*"

"But, Peg, what in the name of God are you talking about?"

"Don't tell me you don't tell the expressmen all about me. Don't tell me you don't drag me down and tell lies about me to the commonest wagonman and chauffeur."

"But, Peggy—"

"Admit it! Admit it! If you were a man you'd admit it."

"Peggy, I haven't been talking . . ."

"If you murdered me in cold blood, you couldn't have wronged me more than you have, Walter Callahan," she said with quivering lips.

X V I I I

He guessed there was nothing to do now but wait for the time to go to bed. Peg was in the bedroom, sewing, making over some of her old clothes. She'd told him she was doing it in order to save him money, and so she would look nice when they went out together. He'd wanted to say that he'd asked her to go out to a movie with him tonight and that she'd refused, but he hadn't because that might have started another quarrel, and he didn't want to fight any more. He just wanted to sit here in peace and quiet and wait until he got sleepy. He was down in the mouth, all right.

He puffed on a cigarette and was very careful about the ashes to be sure that he didn't spill any, because Peg was always bawling him out, saying that he was ruining the rugs with the ashes and making her do extra work. He didn't want to give cause for any more trouble tonight. But, Jesus, he couldn't even spill ashes in his own home. Only today he was talking on the phone with Casey, who used to be one of the clerks in the old days and was now a Dispatcher, and Casey mentioned Porky Mulroy. That went back a long time to the 1920's, when Porky had been Route Inspector. And Casey'd laughed and said the trouble with Porky was that he hadn't worn the pants in his own home. Casey was always saying that about other fellows. But, goddamn it, sitting here alone with himself, could he say that he really wore the pants in his home?

God, everybody who knew Porky was so surprised that you could have knocked them over with a feather when they found out one fine morning that Porky had just picked up and left, throwing over his job and slamming the door on his wife. They'd all laughed and said Porky had given his wife what she had coming to her, but that they hadn't thought Porky had it in him. And then, oh, maybe it was about five years afterward, they heard from some wagonman that Porky had a job running a freight elevator and was hooked up with a young cutie and had even lost weight and was happy. When he'd heard this news, he'd secretly envied Porky, and he'd even imagined doing the same thing himself. He couldn't have walked out because of the kids, Dorothy and Jack. No, that wasn't true. He'd have been afraid to do it, and wouldn't even have known how, or how to find some young girl, or what to say to her if he had found one. And he'd really loved and respected Peg. Yes, he had. But did he still love her?

Hell, he didn't know what he felt about Peg any

more, she kept him off guard and off balance so much. He guessed he was just tired and kind of playing out the schedule. Sometimes his feelings made him think of the White Sox or the St. Louis Browns playing out the schedule in September when they were hopeless in second division.

But why had he suddenly remembered fat Porky Mulroy? He hadn't thought about the Porker in years. It had been like being in another world in the days when he'd known Porky and they'd been young bucks on wagons and then in the Supervision. Everything had changed since then, even in the express business and the Company. There was much more efficiency now, and you had to fill out all kinds of forms and papers and reports, and the young fellows on the trucks talked and thought differently from the way he and Porky and the old-timers had in their days.

But Porky was the man everybody had laughed at because his wife had worn the pants in their home, and Porky had surprised them all by just up and leaving. It was too late for him to do anything like that now.

He suddenly turned and looked to the back of the house. Peg was still quiet. The storm had blown over.

He'd sit here for a while now and think and remember, and then he'd hit the hay.

But what the hell could he do? If he ran off, what kind of a job could he get, and he'd lose his pension, and what could he do? Maybe he could get some kind of a job like a night watchman or running a freight

elevator. Old Simon Murray got a job as night watchman after going on his pension. But all this was just
idle thinking. Who wanted a man his age? What
company or what woman would want a man his age?

A funny nervous feeling was creeping through
him. He often had it. Maybe he was getting the jitters. The house was so quiet now. Peg was still in her
room sewing, and it was peaceful. But he felt as if it
wasn't going to stay peaceful, as if something was going to happen, something was going to happen to
him. He knew that only he and Peg were in the
house, and yet it was as if they weren't alone. He felt
as if he just wanted to run out of the house. He
wanted to be where there was talking and laughing
and you could hear funny stories and laugh right up
from your belly.

What could he do? He was getting all knotted up
inside himself.

X I X

Peg came into the parlor with two glasses of beer.

"I thought you'd like a glass of beer," she said,
speaking very calmly.

Walt was so startled that he didn't react at first.
Then he said:

"Gee, thanks, Peg. A glass of beer would hit the
spot right now."

He took a drink. It tasted good. He'd been thirsty

but he hadn't even realized it while sitting here and thinking, and he was thankful that Peg had come in, and that she was friendly again and had gotten all the nervousness out of her system. Only why couldn't she get it out of her system on Marty the butcher or the men in the supermarket or Mr. Carlton in the drugstore or the neighbors, or on anybody but him?

"Ah," he sighed. "That's good," Walt said, drinking more.

"You can thank me for thinking of you. I always think of you."

"I do, gee, thanks, Peg. It just hits the spot."

"It will relax you," she said, taking a drink herself.

He didn't get that. He didn't think he needed to be relaxed.

"Do you remember that black dress of mine, that old one?"

"Yeh," he said, but as Peg went on describing it his mind wandered and he no longer was listening to her. "Yeh," he repeated.

"You won't know it when you see it on me, the way I'm fixing it up."

"Swell, swell. You know, Peg, you can do things like that mighty well."

"Oh, I'm not so good. You should see what Mrs. Zorobowski down the street can do. But, Walt, when I finish with this dress, it's going to be something that not even Mrs. Zorobowski could do over."

"Gee, that's swell. We can go out to dinner the first

time you wear it and make it the occasion for a celebration."

"Celebration for what?"

"Oh, just to celebrate. After all, Peg, we're not too
old to have a good time."

A few sips of beer had really given him a lift.

"There's nothing to celebrate," Peg said wearily.

Disappointed, he looked at her quizzically.

"Walt, don't you think it's clever of me to make
over an old dress the way I'm doing?"

"Of course, I do, Peg."

"Well, why don't you tell me?"

"But I just did tell you."

"Yes, but only after I had to ask you to."

Walt wondered if he shouldn't make it a rule to
give her more compliments. Hadn't he made a resolution before supper to be more thoughtful and con-
siderate? Did things go bad with Peg because he
didn't show her enough consideration? When they'd
first been married, of course he'd danced attention on
her, but you change and can't be that way all
the time, can you? Well, he was going to be more
thoughtful. And he'd bring her home little presents,
and maybe that would help. Only, bringing home that
Little Gem Syphon hadn't pleased her.

He finished his beer on this thought.

"Here, Walt, let me get you another glass of beer."

He didn't think he ought to have another one. Too
much beer would put on weight. He didn't want to
get fat.

"Oh, I guess one's enough."

Then he remembered that he hadn't said thanks or thank you to her. There he was, right away, right off the reel after making a resolution, forgetting to show her these little attentions.

Peg picked up the two glasses and left the parlor. She quickly returned with the glasses filled.

"Thank you, Peg," he said, as she set one beside him.

"Now, drink your beer and don't sit there sulking at me like a little boy. I only tell you things for your own good."

He smiled. But this kind of talk from Peg didn't really please him. Still, she was being friendly, and she had brought him the beer. And it did taste good, and he didn't feel so down in the mouth now. This second glass would make him feel better, and he could go to bed relaxed and get himself a good night's sleep. But he'd better turn in right after he drank it. Getting up at five-thirty in the morning wasn't easy for a man his age if he didn't get his sleep.

"Walt, I don't want you to fight with me," Peg said, speaking with a ring of sincerity in her voice.

"Peg, why should I want to fight with you?"

"I don't know. I don't know, Walt, but you don't know what it does to me, how it makes me feel."

It didn't make him feel so good, either. He wanted her to know this. But she went on talking.

"If you won't fight and quarrel with me, and if you won't spill ashes and pee on the bathroom floor

73

and not be careless, we'll get along, and I'll be happy and not have any complaints."

Walt smiled sheepishly. She always made him want to crawl into a corner about that bathroom business, and now and then he didn't aim straight, but, God, she exaggerated it all. Still, he wouldn't argue with her, because if you once started she could argue back for hours. Like that night, about three weeks ago, when she'd disputed with him until three o'clock in the morning. He'd gone to work with only two hours sleep. Jack Hartshorn, who relieved him at four o'clock every day, had seen how done in he was and had kidded him, saying:

—What's the matter, Walt, did the old lady take it all out of you last night?—

He'd grinned, letting Jack believe that was the reason he was so bushed. Sure, his old lady had done him in and taken it all out of him, but not the way Jack had imagined but by arguing with him until his tongue had been almost hanging out.

"Tell me, Walt, aren't you sorry?"

Walt didn't want to say it, but it was the easiest thing for him to do.

"Yes, Peg."

"And you're not going to start any more fights with me?"

They drank their beer. It tasted very good to Walt. "Oh, another glass of beer won't hurt you in the least," Peg said.

"How about you, Peg?"

Peg pointed to her glass beside her; it was more than half full. Then she took his glass out to the kitchen to refill it.

Sometimes when she would wait on him this way, she would suddenly snap at him then and blame him. But she wasn't that way now. She was in one of her best moods. Maybe they could have a good time just sitting here and talking. If they did, it sure would be worth it to lose a few hours' sleep.

"Why aren't you always the way you are now, Walt?" she asked him as she returned with another glass of beer.

"But, Peg, I want to be. I don't want to quarrel."

"And do you think I do? All I think of is you. I want to take care of you. At your time of life a man needs to be careful about himself, and you know, Walt, you never did know how to take care of yourself."

Walt wanted to talk about other things. This subject made him too uneasy. But, still, it did please him to think that she'd say these things. He guessed she really cared for him. Maybe she got so nervous because she worried about him. Of late he'd been thinking again and again that she no longer loved him, that she didn't care if he did or didn't enjoy any little happiness during the rest of his life. But when she talked this way about taking care of him, well, yes, it did please him mightily, even if it did seem that she was telling him at the same time that he wasn't so much of a man.

He took another drink of beer.

And her voice, as she talked to him now, was soft, and maybe there was love in it. Underneath everything else she was still Peg, the girl and the woman he'd loved. When they were young, he used to love her voice, her voice and her hair. Her voice had seemed so soft and gentle to him, so feminine, and he remembered that secretly he used to call it the voice of love itself. God, wouldn't he have gotten the real Bronx cheer and the razzle-dazzle, though, from the fellows at the Express Company if he'd ever told them he had such thoughts? But her voice did make him remember.

She was talking softly to him now, and he was only half listening, and he was feeling as if he might almost be in a dream, although he knew it wasn't a dream, but it was almost like being in a dream, the way he was feeling, with Peg talking to him, her voice seeming soft and, yes, like it was when he first had known her. And he was thinking of her hair, too. *When your hair has turned to silver.* . . . There was gray in her hair now, and it was kind of stringy, the black hair that once, once upon a time, he had loved. He used to love to look at it, and to feel it and stroke it and put his face into it and smell it and kiss it.

There was a soft look in his eyes. He drained his third glass of beer.

"One more beer won't hurt you, Walt. It will be good for you," she said solicitously.

He wanted to tell her that he had had enough, but he didn't.

She left the parlor with the empty glass.

Peg had not finished even her second glass.

X X

"Peg, I'm not such a bad fellow, I'm not," Walt exclaimed, his voice thick and pleading.

He was feeling good, in a good mood. He wanted to talk, wanted to tell Peg about himself so she'd understand that he was decent, and that he went along as well as the next fellow did, with his shoulder to the wheel. He wanted her to know this.

He couldn't remember how many glasses of beer he'd drunk, but it was more than he'd had in one hell of a long time. But then he was safe. Nothing could happen to him because he was right here in his own home, drinking with Peg. And Peg wasn't sore at him about drinking now, as she'd been sometimes when he'd gotten tanked up. In fact, she was serving him the beer, so it was all right. Peg was letting him drink. Hadn't she told him it would be good for him? And Peg could put him to bed, and she wouldn't nag him about it, either, because she'd told him to do it. Why, she was drinking a glass of beer herself.

Peg wasn't a spring chicken any more, but, then, he wasn't young himself. She had given him the best of her. He did care for her, and that was why this quarreling and haggling and nagging bothered him so much. But they weren't quarreling and fighting now, and they could make up. Peg was in a good mood, and he could see that she didn't mean a lot of the things she said. Why, he and Peg were even having a good time together right here in their own home. Think of that!

"A few glasses of beer will be good for you, so long as you don't get sick and pass out," Peg said, placing another glass on the small table beside him.

"I'm not drunk. I'm not gonna get drunk and get sick and pass . . . pass out," Walt said, speaking slowly but confidently.

Peg sipped her beer. Walt gulped his.

"Why, after all, don't I have to get up . . . and get to work early . . . in the mornin'?"

"I bought all of this beer today," she said. "I just thought I ought to have it in the house for you."

This pleased him. It proved that Peg did think of him and of what he liked. Peg could be mighty good and sweet—yes, she could when she wasn't in one of her nervous moods. No, sir, knowing her, he wouldn't trade her for any other man's wife, no, sir. And he understood her.

Walt grinned foolishly. Peg, watching him and noticing his grin, frowned briefly.

"And I bought Schlitz beer, because I know it's the beer you like best."

Peg looked down at her partially empty glass. She was moving her legs with nervous regularity. He noticed her legs. They were still nice and shapely. Yes, she still had good legs.

He told himself that he really felt very sympathetic to Peg. After all, she was growing old, just as he was. And wasn't it harder on a woman to grow old and lose her looks and her figure than it was on a man? Yes, it was, it was sadder for a woman. He must remember this and make allowances for Peg. After all, words were only words, and when she was a little upset he ought to try to keep cool and wait for the storm to blow over. Because the nervous, nagging Peg wasn't really Peg. Peg, sitting there before him drinking beer with him, she was the real Peg.

"I was thinkin', Peg . . . I was thinkin' we've gone through a lot together . . . haven't we . . . Peg, old girl?"

He saw the dark look on her face. It frightened him a little. What had he said? Then he guessed that maybe it was because he'd called her "old girl."

"It's been hard on me, and you know, Walt, you haven't always been as attentive and careful as you might have been."

The dark look vanished from her face. Her voice was soft and low and friendly.

"I tried to, Peg. I have. I . . . think I can honestly . . . honestly say I tried to be . . . careful and . . . attentive and to be a good . . . husband. And I always . . . work, and I think I can honestly say . . . I worked . . . hard."

Walt wanted to say more. He wanted to tell Peg

79

that now he sometimes felt the years of work and the onset of age. But, the hell with it, the hell with it. Why should he think of this now, when he was having a good time?

Walt drained his glass of beer.

Then he looked at the empty glass. He wanted another, but he didn't know whether or not he should have it, and he didn't know if Peg would like it. He didn't dare ask her for fear she might say no. But he had this thirst for another beer. What the hell, another glass wouldn't hurt him.

Suddenly he got up and lurched to the bathroom. He determined to aim straight, but he didn't. Panicky and perspiring, he snatched wads of toilet paper and bent down to wipe up the floor where some of his urine had hit. He didn't want her to be telling him about it. It humiliated him. The odor depressed and almost sickened him. He felt humiliated anyway. God, if any of his friends at work saw him now and should know why he was doing this, wouldn't they lay it into him?

He wiped up the floor sloppily and got more wads of toilet paper and did it over again. He didn't like this, getting some of it on his fingers. He dropped the wads into the toilet bowl, pulled the chain, and anxiously washed his hands. Then, after drying them, he saw that all the paper hadn't been flushed down. He got panicky and pulled the chain again. He waited tensely. One wad still hadn't gone down. He waited in growing panic for the bowl to refill so that he could flush it again. Then he flushed it a third time. The last wad went down. He was safe. He sighed with relief. He shyly went back to the parlor, walking with a slight stagger and trying to think of what he would tell Peg if she asked him questions or criticized him for having been in the bathroom so long, and for having pulled the chain three times, in case she'd heard the toilet flushing.

Peg sat waiting for him, a beaming smile on her face. She had placed another glass of beer on the table beside his chair.

"You're not sick, are you?"

"No, no, not at all."

"You were in the bathroom so long."

"I had to be," he said, embarrassed.

He sat down and, feigning surprise at seeing another glass of beer, said:

"Gee, thanks for pouring my beer, Peg."

"I thought another glass wouldn't hurt you."

He needn't have sweated and worried about what Peg would say.

"No, it won't hurt me. It's the last glass I'll drink tonight. And then I'm gonna turn in."

Peg hadn't finished her second glass of beer yet.

X X I

Walt staggered out of the bathroom. He hadn't aimed straight, but, the hell with it, he thought.

He told himself he was drunk. Immediately, he corrected himself. He wasn't drunk. He could still hold his beer. He wasn't drunk. He was just a little drunk.

He lumbered into the parlor and dropped heavily into his chair. He tried to remember what he'd been talking about to Peg, but it had gone from his mind. He'd been telling her about himself, something important about himself. But whatever it was, it had slipped his mind.

He lurched as he picked up his glass and gulped the beer in it. He wanted more immediately.

"Peg, can I have another glass of . . . beer?"

"You're drunk already, and you have to go to work tomorrow. Why, your tongue is thick. You're talking like a drunken man."

"I'm not drunk . . . just feeling good."

"You can't control yourself. You've been running to the bathroom every two minutes."

"You got to go to bathroom, the bathroom . . ." He lost the thread of what he was saying. A puzzled, stupid expression came over his face. Then, and as though with an effort, he said, "Yourself."

"When you get drunk, the real animal, the beast you are comes out," she said cruelly.

"What the hell you talking about?"

"You know what I'm talking about, Walt Callahan! You know good and well."

He hiccupped. He knew he ought to go to bed. Go to bed and sleep. Tomorrow. Work. It was late. Late. He was sleepy.

He hiccupped again.

Sleep. He was getting drunk. Getting drunk.

He stared at the empty beer glass.

He lumbered to his feet.

"I'm gonna . . . have another beer."

She jumped up and snatched his glass.

"Don't you take my glass."

"I'm only getting you the beer," she said in an angry voice; she was almost in tears.

She strode out of the parlor. He looked after her, puzzled.

He yawned. He hiccupped.

Damn her! He was going to show her who wore the pants in this family. Trouble with too many women, they wanted to wear the pants.

Peg came back smiling. She set the beer down before him.

"You wouldn't have this beer to drink if I hadn't thought of you and ordered it today. I paid a boy fifteen cents to carry it home for me. I couldn't carry it myself."

"I paid for it."

"I'll be busy all day tomorrow cleaning up the drunken mess you've made tonight."

Walt took the glass and drank. He wiped his lips with the back of his hand.

"Now, what you say?" he said, sitting down.

He sat, slumped in an ungainly position, with his mouth hanging open.

X X I I

Lying in the darkness, on the outside of the bed, Walt smelled of beer and sweat. Peg was beside him. He knew she was sore at him. He mumbled to himself that she was all he had now. He wanted to make up to her. He wanted to make love to her. He didn't want her to be sore at him.

"You'd still be swilling beer like a pig in the trough if there was any left to drink," Peg said bitterly.

"I only drank . . . drank . . . all I did."

"That's what I get for my thoughtfulness and consideration. And he gets drunk. I have to sleep with a pig. Why don't you bring a horse in my bed and let it drop horse turds on my pillow?"

"Peg . . . I love . . . you," he muttered feebly.

"Love! I suppose you drank so much beer that you'll wet the bed."

Walt passed out and began to snore. He didn't hear another word she said as she sat up in bed beside him, berating him.

X X I I I

The streetcar was crowded. How had he gotten on the streetcar? He didn't know. And how would he get through the day's work? He didn't know.

84

Luckily, he had gotten a seat. If he had to hang on a strap this morning, he couldn't take it.

His head!

What a goddamned fool he had been, drinking so much beer.

His head!

And it was hard trying to keep his eyes open.

The car was bumping along, getting more crowded at each stop. The conductor was barking at the passengers.

He had trouble keeping his eyes open. He felt bloated.

And his head!

As soon as he got down to the Depot, he'd send out for coffee.

God, why had he done it? It hadn't been any fun. But Peg had let him drink all that beer. Why hadn't she stopped him? Why hadn't she just put her foot down and not gone on giving him more? Peg shouldn't have let him do it.

His head!

He remembered getting into bed and Peg sore at him and himself passing out and Peg saying something about horses and . . .

His head!

Walt fell asleep in the crowded streetcar.

X X I V

Peg didn't want to get up and look at the mess Walt had made in the parlor. Cleaning his mess, that was what her life had come to.

She didn't know what time it was. She didn't care. She didn't want to get up and face the day. Oh, God, she hated to wake up in the morning. Every morning, waking up to face the day.

He had gone to work. Some Express wives got up at five or six in the morning and cooked their husbands' breakfast. But maybe those wives had husbands who appreciated it.

She laughed loudly, several times.

Imagine, she told herself, any expressman appreciating what his wife did for him. But some of them didn't have wives, they had slaves. Wasn't that what he wanted her to be—his slave? He treated her like a slave.

She was nervous and disgusted. She wished she could sleep. But, ox that he was, he had wakened her when he got out of bed. And the alarm clock. It rang in her ears. It rang so that she wanted to break it, smash it, smash it to smithereens. She wanted to smash every alarm clock in the world. Every morning, the alarm clock woke her up, and she couldn't get back to sleep.

She turned over on her side and sniffled. Then the tears came. She sobbed, and her body quivered and shook. She moaned. She groaned. She exclaimed loudly:

"Oh! Oh! Oh!"

She kicked her legs. She flailed her arms. With her thighs pressed together tightly, she lay with her body stretched and taut, and a nameless fear took hold of her. It seemed as though the fears that gripped her were presences hovering in the room. She had goose pimples. She shivered and shuddered, wanting to scream out. She imagined she did scream, but she remained rigid and silent. Then she imagined the seeming presences in the darkened bedroom would speak to her and accuse her.

She heard nothing.

X X V

Walt Callahan stood in his small Dispatcher's booth, looking at the pail of coffee set before him on the built-in desk. It was cluttered with papers. Outside, the Depot was noisy. It was stacked with all kinds of freight. Trailers and trucks were backed up side by side against the platform. Walt often liked to describe this by saying the vehicles were backed against the loading platform ass by ass. Freight handlers were bustling about, lugging, pushing, wheeling, and sorting freight. Wagonmen with uniform caps were sidling in and out of the freight on the platform, talking, standing near their vehicles. Route Inspectors were moving around, giving instructions to their men about the morning deliveries. A tractor backed into a trailer with a clang, hooked it on, and in a moment, its motor sputtering, it was noisily moving out. There was bustle, clatter, shouting of voices, crashing sounds, all mingling into a roar. But this was all so familiar to him. Most mornings he hardly heard it, or, even when he did, it was almost as if he didn't hear it, it was so usual. Today it beat in on him, and the whole Depot was like one goddamn madhouse.

He hoped the coffee would wake him and pick him up. God, would four o'clock ever come? Usually, time passed so fast, it flew by. And on those days he didn't want time to fly by so fast, because at the end of the day there was home, going home. He often didn't want to leave because he never knew what Peg would be like. But he felt sick today. The coffee. It was brown. The brown color was pretty. He looked at the coffee.

He took a gulp from the small tin pail. After it went down, he held his breath for a moment, waiting to discover if it helped. He looked through the smudgy window of his booth, and everything seemed blurred for a moment. He didn't know if he could last out the day. His head was still aching, but the aspirin he'd taken was helping a little. Now it was mostly tiredness. He took another gulp of coffee. How could he get through the day?

X X V I

Wearing her bathrobe, and with her hair tangled and uncombed, Peg was an aging, haggard, tortured-looking woman. There was no makeup on her thin face. There were hollows under her eyes. They shone brightly, and their gaze was fixed. The lines about her mouth seemed more pronounced than usual, and her hands and wrists looked almost scrawny.

She stared into the mirror over the mantelpiece and saw a confused image of a woman younger than herself, with a face less marked by years and suffering than her own. She saw a rather handsome face crowned with black hair untouched by gray. She saw round, rosy cheeks and passionate, glittering, dark eyes. She saw herself as a beautiful woman, and in the mirror the twisted, weird smile on her face was charming and gracious. She put her right hand over her face and continued to stare between her fingers for some moments. She hummed the tune of a song with a title and words that she had forgotten.

She turned and stared rigidly about the parlor, gazing as though she saw something very interesting. She ran her hand through her hair, mussing it more and making it look even more wild and weedy.

She shuddered and trembled with fear. It seemed to her that she was about to do something terrible, and she didn't even know what it was.

"Oh, why doesn't he hit me over the head and tell

me to stop it . . . stop it! . . stop it!" she cried out plaintively to the empty room.

Then she shook her head, and her face relaxed. She was sleepy, half asleep, she told herself. She was only waking up. She had been dreaming on her feet. And last night she'd had some horrible dream she couldn't remember, except that she was standing over a dead man and that she was filled with horror.

She shuddered as she remembered even this much of her dream.

—Oh, how can I face this day? she silently asked herself.

And look at the room. It was filthy, worse than a stable or a pigpen. And the odor of tobacco and stale beer was enough to make a woman ill. A newspaper lay on the floor near Walt's chair, and there were ashes all over the rug. The ash tray on the small table beside her chair was filled, and the one on the table next to his was overflowing, with ashes on the table, too. And there were two beer glasses on one end. She became furious and said aloud:

"I've never seen such a filthy room in my life."

She turned and went out to the kitchen to drink her morning coffee.

X X V I I

Walt didn't have time to stop and know how he felt. The morning rush was on, and the Depot was all excitement, noise, bustle, and confusion. He stood in his booth, giving orders to drivers who came and went, talking to Route Inspectors, speaking on the telephone, thinking about the loads he had to get out in order to clean up for the morning. Everything looked as if it were in disorder, but to Walt it wasn't. He knew what he was doing, what drivers he would pick for loads, and that in another hour or hour and a half he'd have the Depot platform clean as a whistle and ready to receive the trailers that would be coming in with transfer loads. He got a kick out of his work, having a whole Depot full of freight to get out, watching and knowing that it would go, load by load, cleaning it out so that the Depot would be cleared and dull and empty. And it wasn't as hard as it seemed. Hell, he'd been dispatching so long that he could just about do it in his sleep.

And when he worked under pressure, he didn't have time to think about himself or about home and Peg. He lost himself here in these details of work. He saw lots of people, some of them friends of his. He got on well with most of them, didn't have serious trouble with his own drivers, and usually he just felt good here on the platform and in his Dispatcher's booth. And he liked the noise and activity, the shouts of the billers sometimes rising singsong above the crashing noise of boxes, and he liked to see the platform men going by carrying and pushing the freight. He got a thrill out of his work. Yes, it gave him a sense of being connected with a big undertaking that was important in the life of the country, the moving of freight.

This morning he was pleased about his work. He was holding up after having come in this morning with a hangover. Everything was going along just as usual. And he was doing his job even though he was fagged out. He'd pepped himself up with coffee, and the aspirin was working, taking away his headache. And, damn it, that was pretty good for a man his age. It was! Hell, he'd even thought of calling up and saying he was sick and not coming down today. He would have done it except that he'd been afraid Peg would have been on his tail at home all day, nagging and telling him how drunk he'd been. He was glad he hadn't stayed home. He'd just have had a lousy day, and maybe Peg would have carried on, telling him how women were stronger than men and she was stronger than he was. That was what she'd done the last time he'd been home sick, last winter when he'd had that touch of the flu.

Bobby Dickson, who wrote sheets for him, came into the booth. Bobby was sandy-haired, short, cheerful, and always smiling.

"Walt, Mr. Tuttle the Depot Foreman told me . . ."

"What's eating his ass this morning? He was sober last night, not drunk like me."

"He told me to tell you you're slipping!"

Walt made a waving gesture of dismissal with his left hand.

"His old lady gave him hell again maybe for takin' a pee."

Somehow, he got pleasure out of thinking that Tuttle was henpecked. If they knew here at the Company how much he was, they'd be surprised.

"The point is, Walt, I have a message I am instructed to deliver to you from Mr. Tuttle, the . . . say, what the hell is his title again, I plumb forgot it?"

"Depot Foreman. And I know what's on his mind—them two stiffs. Well, here, take this pail and run across the street and get me some coffee and tell him that cars are on the way in to get them. Heinie Mueller promised me he'd get them for me."

"He always gets this way about getting stiffs delivered. I told him that's because he's a brother of theirs and likes to do well by his family."

"What did he say?" Walt asked, laughing.

"He said that if I was in workin' for him I'd be out of work."

Walt chuckled.

"He's dead, a brother to a stiff. All right, Bobby, get me the java and tell Mr. Tuttle to find something else to worry about, now that I've got his two brothers in coffins well provided for."

"Okay, Walt."

Bobby took the coffee pail and hopped out of the booth.

Suddenly Walt felt tired and depressed. He

dropped onto his chair. Those stiffs he had to get delivered. Some day he'd be a stiff. That would be all for him, and he'd just be a stiff, forgotten, except maybe now and then when someone remembered him the way he would now and then remember and think about Patsy McLaughlin and Jim O'Neill and Mike Mulrooney and Billie O'Brien and Gas-House McGinty. And . . .

He lit a cigarette to clear his head and wake himself up. He wished Bobby would hurry back with the coffee.

"Mr. Callahan," said Tommy Gustav, one of his drivers.

Walt looked up.

"What the hell do you want?" Walt asked with mock gruffness.

"Jesus Christ, I always get the toughest loads. When am I ever going to get a break, Mr. Callahan?"

"Come on, Gustav, come on, quit feeling sorry for yourself. When I was your age, you should have seen the loads I used to haul. And the hours I put in."

"I know that's maybe so. My old man killed himself workin' in a steel mill, too. But I don't want that. I believe in progress for a workin'man."

"Hell, and look at the pay you get. God, we didn't begin to draw down pay like you boys do."

"It's not so much when you have a family. I came down last payday with a dime in my pocket, and there wasn't a cent at home."

"Well, Gustav, what's your beef?"

"I'm late feedin' every day. Then I catch hell from Martinov, my boss, because I get on my routes late. I got twenty minutes overtime last night, and he burned my ass off, burned it right clean off me this mornin'."

"If you didn't jaw so much, you wouldn't be late gettin' on your route. Your loads are no heavier than a lot of others I got to dish out here every mornin'. Boy, my job is to get freight out of the Depot. And what's your truck for?"

"Well, I do the best I can, and I don't see why Martinov should burn me."

"Hey, Walt! How you doin'?" a fat driver called cheerfully as he passed Walt's booth.

"Hello, Charlie," Walt called back with a wave of his hand.

"Yes, all I ask is a break."

"All right, boy—get on the ball, and I'll see what I can do for you tomorrow mornin'. And tell Martinov to see me about your mornin' loads. You work for me in the mornin'. I'll take care of him if he burns you up again. Hell, I was dispatchin' when he was a punk on a single wagon in the old days."

"Thanks, Mr. Callahan."

"Walt's the name."

"Thanks, Walt."

Walt watched Gustav leave the booth. He was a strapping young fellow, strong and decent, too. What was the kid's home life like?

Walt suddenly thought of the time when he was as

young as Gustav. But the phone in his booth rang, breaking into the mood of nostalgia which came upon him.

X X V I I I

Peg was on her knees, slowly scrubbing the bathroom floor, thinking how she'd scrubbed it yesterday, and only because of Walt she had to do it all over again. He made her do it almost every day because of his filthy habits. But now the smell was gone. She smelled only soap and water. She liked the smell of soap. It was a clean smell. She liked clean smells because she was a clean woman.

But would Walt ever stop? Did he care how hard she worked? For twenty years, for more than twenty years, for all the years of their life together, she had asked him, she had pleaded with him, she had begged him and begged him and begged him about the bathroom floor. He did it only to make her get down on her knees and scrub. He had taken ten years off her life and her beauty just by making her scrub the bathroom floor.

Her face looked anguished. Her hair fell over her forehead. She perspired. She felt aches in her arms and cramps in her legs. Her knees hurt. She scrubbed the floor forlornly.

—Scrubbing your piss, she said aloud to the grinning, hateful image of her husband that rose in her mind.

X X I X

"I'll tell you, Heinie," Walt said into the telephone mouthpiece, "I had too much beer last night."

"I can't do that any more, not on a night when I got to get up and come down here to work the next morning."

"Hell, Heinie, you been up there in that department so long you could run things in your sleep. How long you been in the Wagon Department, Heinie? Since Father Time was born?"

"I been here since I came back from the War in 1918."

"Jesus, that war. It sounds like the Civil War to me."

"What did your old lady say about you drinkin', Walt?"

"She was with me."

"Did she get drunk, too?" Heinie asked enthusiastically.

"No, Heinie, she just took care of me. I had such a good time, though, Heinie, that I don't mind the hangover," Walt explained, thinking of how he was giving such a different impression of what had happened than what was really so. "And, Heinie, you know I feel pretty chipper despite all I drank. Send over one of your lumber heads from the Department so I can knock on wood. I'm doing pretty good, Heinie, at my age."

"I'm in good shape, Walt, except for my dogs. How's your dogs, Walt?"

"Pretty good, Heinie, pretty good. I'm on them more than you, and they bother me now and then, but not too much. Yep, Heinie, the dogs are holdin' pretty good."

"I'm glad to hear that, Walt; you and I are among the few old-timers left now."

"That's so."

"And I tell you, Walt, we're lucky because of our ladies. Your old woman, Walt, and mine are too good to shoot." Heinie let out a cackling laugh. "When you get along in years like we are, Walt, and you begin to have dogs like an old man's pecker, the old lady you got makes all the difference in the world, and we got old girls to be proud of."

"Yes, Heinie, I'm with you on that proposition," Walt answered.

"I took care of your stiffs, too. The cars are on the way to pick 'em up."

"Thanks, Heinie, you're a prince. And it'll take Tuttle off my neck."

"Say, is he still livin'?"

"He's worse than he ever was, Heinie."

"Well, Walt, any time you need a car to take care of him the way I'm takin' care of those two stiffs of yours this morning, you know who to call."

They both laughed.

"Well, keep up the good work, Walt."

"Same for you, Heinie, and remember me to the old lady."

"And same to yours, Walt."

They hung up. Walt stood in his booth for a moment. An overpowering sadness came upon him. He was thinking of Heinie Mueller. Heinie was growing old here in the Express Company, a happier man than he. And it was because Heinie had a different wife. Heinie, none of the men down here in the Company, knew what his home life was like. He didn't want them to know. They all thought he was a jolly, happy man, and he didn't want them to think anything else, but, still . . .

"Walt, you got to come out and see about that trailer load Stoneman's takin' to Atlantic," Bobby said at the entrance to the booth.

"Okay."

Walt followed Bobby onto the platform. He still felt despair in his heart. And suddenly he was weak. His hangover was coming back on him.

X X X

"Mother, you really ought to fix yourself up," Dorothy said, as she and Peg sat talking in the parlor.

Dorothy had brown hair, blue eyes, full lips, and a round, pleasant face. She was beginning to look stout and gave the appearance of being very contented.

99

"What is there for me to fix up for?" Peg asked in an emotionless tone of voice.

Dorothy became uneasy. Her mother seemed a little foolish, and she looked awful, like the wrath of God. But she told herself she'd better be careful about what she said, because she didn't want to argue. Her attitude toward her mother kept changing. At times she was angry with her and disliked her. They had even quarreled violently and bitterly. And her mother had been very spiteful and unfriendly when she and Joe had gotten married. But Joe was such an understanding, tolerant kind of person. Then she and her mother had a long, terrible quarrel, but they had made up, and she was glad they had. Now she didn't quarrel with her mother, and if she did, she always felt badly about it. Dorothy always had believed you should respect your mother, and now that she was a mother herself, she felt this more strongly. But every time she got to feeling too sorry about her own mother, to thinking she shouldn't criticize her mother, then something would happen and she would have to control herself so as not to become angry all over again. And a deep, silent resentment of her mother would burn in her. But then she would tell herself it was all past and was best forgotten. You couldn't be happy if you kept raking up the past and brooding about it. Sometimes she'd remember how her mother used to scream at her and nag her when she'd been a child, and she'd recall scenes when she thought she'd even hated her mother. Her mother hadn't done much to give her a happy childhood. But she really forgave her for everything.

But today Dorothy felt genuinely sorry for Peg. She had come over and brought her mother a nice blouse as a present and she had a tie for her father. Her mother had not seemed in the least pleased by the gift and had said that Walt wouldn't look well in the tie. This had disappointed Dorothy. But, despite this, she was determined to be friendly with her mother and to try to cheer up the poor thing.

"Your father was drunk last night. I spent all morning cleaning up after him."

"Where did he go—out with some of the boys from the Express Company?"

"He turned my home here into a saloon."

"What did he do?" Dorothy asked.

"He turned the parlor and the bathroom into a stable. You'd think he was a horse and wanted to pass his water wherever he was, just the way a horse does on the street."

"Mother!" Dorothy exclaimed, shocked.

This almost sickened Dorothy. She suddenly remembered that Joe had often said her old man ought to leave that old lady of hers, and that if the old lady kicked off first, her father could always find a home with them.

"You know your father. You know how hard I worked bringing up you children."

Dorothy was puzzled. She just could not understand how her mother could say any such thing. After all, she remembered very well how her mother had always nagged and bawled out her father, and given him so little peace, and she remembered, too, many times her father had been kind and had brought home presents and candy for her mother, as well as for Jack and herself. Her father had been very good to all of them. Her mother was just not telling the truth. This pained her. She felt sorry, too, very sorry, to think that her mother got things so twisted up.

And she suddenly realized that Mother had always been this way; she had always had a chip on her shoulder and been too nervous and too inclined to feel sorry for herself, and to expect too much from Father and from others. She just wished that there were something she could say or do. But what? And Mother looked old and so tired. She wished she could only help to make things easier here for her father, and, yes, for her mother, too.

"How can a woman live with a man like that?" Peg asked in a very sad voice.

Dorothy recalled that her mother had once asked the same question about herself and Joe.

"Mother, a wife has to be sensible. A man has to blow off steam. I know that. Because I know Joe. Joe has got to blow off steam, and so when he does I let him. I get him the beer and I let him drink it. Then he goes to bed, and the next day he feels a little sorry, and he is even kinder than usual to me and to the children."

"Yes, Joe is wonderful, Dorothy; you have a wonderful husband," Peg said.

"Just let Father drink his beer now and then and go to bed and sleep it off. Father never did anyone any harm. And baby him a little, Mother, at times. All men like a little babying."

"Dorothy, I do nothing else. I have to baby him all the time. You don't know your father any more. He's a grouchy old man now. You say those things because I . . . I brought you up to love him. I was on my knees until they were red and raw, I was on my knees until they ached, scrubbing the bathroom floor."

Dorothy was too deeply hurt and saddened to answer her mother. If she were alone now, she would cry. And she was afraid there was no use trying to talk sensibly to her mother.

"No, your father's not well. He's not well. I do my best to take care of him. I always did my best. Does he care? Does he appreciate it?"

"What's the matter with Father?" Dorothy asked in alarm.

Peg's eyes changed. A sudden light of understanding came into them.

"After all, he's an old man, and staying up late, drinking the way he did last night, and than having to get up at the crack of dawn isn't good for a man. But it's not my fault."

"But, Mother, is there anything wrong with Father?"

"He coughed last night in his sleep. What with his coughing and snoring, I didn't get a wink of sleep myself."

"Then you should rest today, Mother."

"Who's going to clean up your father's mess if I lie in bed all day?"

"Oh, Mother, please be sensible," Dorothy said.

Her sense of alarm about her father's health was gone. She decided that her mother had been exaggerating again and just getting things wrong.

"You can talk after I raised you! You don't have to live with him! You can talk, Dorothy. Because you don't know. You'll never know. You'll never know the kind of a man I have lived with!"

"Mother, you expect too much of Father. He was a hard-working man. He still is. He kept one job with the same company for years. My goodness, Mother, what can you expect of a man?"

"You don't know your father as I do," Peg said with finality. Then, after a pause, and with strain in her voice, she added, "You'll never know your father as I have known him."

Dorothy restrained her anger.

Peg seemed to sense that she might have said too much. She had said many things to Dorothy about what a brute Dorothy's husband, Joe, was, and this had caused trouble between her and her daughter, and now she very much wanted Dorothy on her side against Walt. Her children were all she had left in the world to live for, her children and her grandchildren.

"Come, Dorothy, let me make you a cup of tea."

"Oh, don't bother, Mother."

"It's no bother at all. I was just going to make myself some anyway," Peg said sweetly.

Dorothy nodded her head. She felt just hopelessly sad about Mother.

X X X I

Walt sat at the counter of the crowded, noisy restaurant, having a bowl of chicken soup. On most days he didn't go out for lunch at all but just sent over for sandwiches and coffee and went right on working. He used to bring his lunch, but Peg had made so much fuss about making it that he stopped taking it so he wouldn't have to hear her talk about it. But on his lunch hour did he have to think of that? He had come here just to get away from the Depot and to pass the time, hoping this would fortify him for the rest of the day.

The soup was just what he needed. When he'd first looked at the steaming bowl, he hadn't wanted to touch it. But the first spoonful felt good, and now he was lapping it up. It was hitting the right spot, too. Catching the eye of the counterman, he said:

"Good soup."

The counterman frowned. Walt asked himself what that poor guy's trouble was.

There were a number of express drivers in the restaurant, and they and the other customers were talking and laughing, and the place was very gay. Down the counter from him, one young driver, Dick Tappins, was saying:

"Yes, and so the poor sonofabitch is putting all that dough into insurance so his wife will be provided for if he kicks the bucket. We was having beers at the tavern where I go, out my way, and he was telling us. Hell, he's been telling us this story so damned many times I know what he's going to say by heart, once he says something about his insurance. So I says to him, I says, 'Listen, you'll do without things, break your back working, and then you'll croak and your wife will be picked up by the first bum she meets in the tavern, and that bum will get all the fruits of your labor.' "

Dick Tappins let out a healthy laugh. A couple of drivers beside him laughed with him.

Walt grinned and went on drinking his soup. He remembered how he often had laughed like that. He didn't seem to laugh as much nowadays. He guessed that as you started to get on in years, maybe you just lost the ability to laugh as much. But, hell, hadn't he been a young fellow once like Dick Tappins, full of beans and energy? He never thought his life could turn out to be the kind of a life it was. But, then, no life ever did. Only he never thought that things would be the way they were with himself and Peg. It made you sad.

There was more loud talk and laughter. He caught snatches of it and smiled at some of the jokes he overheard. He wanted to swing around on the stool and holler out some jokes or make some cracks himself, but he didn't. Once there hadn't been a man in the Express Company who liked a joke better than he. Hell, today the jokes just weren't in him. He felt very lonely in the gay restaurant.

X X X I I

Walt was making a determined effort to eat a hot roast-beef sandwich with gravy and mashed potatoes. When you had a hangover, you had to get some food in you and pick up your energy and spirits. He was relieved about one thing, too. Physically, he must be pretty much okay, because he had gotten through the morning, he was putting away a good lunch, and he was starting to feel as if maybe he might be up to par.

When Walt saw Stratton, a driver, take a seat beside him, his spirits dropped. Stratton was a decent enough fellow, and did his work well and minded his own business, only he was such a depressed fellow that you didn't want him around.

Stratton was small and thin, and he looked harassed and weazened. He was in his late thirties, and his hair had already begun to grow gray at the temples.

"Hello, Mr. Callahan," Stratton said spiritlessly.

"Why, hello, Stratton. Who you workin' for these days?"

"Mr. Moylan."

"Well, old Troubles himself. He's still going strong. And how's tricks with you, young fellow?"

"You'll never get rich with a family."

"Yes, you've got a big family. Well, you'll have support when you grow old."

"My wife's pregnant again."

"Boy, you never stop. What will this make?"

"Seven."

"And you only making a driver's salary. I should think you'd call it a day as far as populatin' the world goes, Stratton."

"My wife won't let me."

"Won't let you what?"

"Won't let me stop."

Walt laughed.

"You got a gal who likes it. That's what gals and wives are for."

"It's against her religion to let me do anything. You're a Catholic, aren't you, Mr. Callahan?"

"Yes, of course I am."

"Does the Church demand it that way?"

"Well, I'll tell you, Stratton, I ain't up much on my catechism, but I stopped and took precautions."

Stratton stared at Walt in disbelief.

"And your wife let you?"

"Sure, she did," Walt said breezily.

"Gee, your wife must be different from mine," Stratton said.

Walt was touched. He wasn't the only man in the world who got a rough going from his old lady, he thought to himself. Stratton must have it worse than he did. Look at the poor lad, washed out, dried up, looking as if there wasn't any spirit left in him, and he wasn't forty yet.

"How is the wife?" Walt asked.

"Oh, I don't know, Mr. Callahan. I came home from work the other night and the house was dirty, and the kids were hungry and crying, and my supper wasn't ready. I asked my wife what was the matter. She said to me that God hadn't told her that day to take care of the kids and cook their supper and my supper. She keeps telling me what God tells her to do and what God doesn't tell her to do."

Stratton's voice sounded hopeless. He talked like a bewildered man. Walt, listening to him, was surprised. He didn't like to believe the thought that had come to him as Stratton went on talking about his wife. This poor loogin Stratton must have a crazy wife. God, Peg wasn't that bad. No, Peg wasn't like that. She knew what she was doing, and she didn't talk to God. Stratton was much worse off than he was.

Walt finished his lunch. Stratton just got him down too much for Walt to want to talk to him. He wanted to get away. He felt sorry for the poor guy, but what could he do to help him?

Christ, what can I do to help myself? he asked himself.

"Well, it's a tough life if you don't weaken," Stratton said.

"Yes," Walt said, getting down from the stool at the counter.

"Keep your pecker up, lad," he said sympathetically, giving Stratton a friendly pat on the shoulder.

Then, as he walked away toward the cash desk to pay his check, he suddenly reflected that what Stratton had to do, more than anything else, was not to keep his pecker up. Walt laughed at his own joke but without zest.

X X X I I I

With a toothpick between his teeth, Walt stood outside the restaurant. Little Willie Collins sidled up to him. He wore an express cap with a badge on it. His face was ruddy and his hair was graying.

"Hi, Walt."

"Why, hello, Willie. Feedin'?"

"Yes."

Willie stood looking up at Walt for a moment. Walt knew what was coming.

"Walt, when do you think they're going to call me back?"

"Hell, Willie, I don't know. Every year the emphasis is on more efficiency, and it looks as if they'll keep cutting down the number of Route Inspectors and Dispatchers."

"I know, but no man who knows me doesn't know that I got a rough deal. You know how good I was when I was Chief Dispatcher up in the Call Department in the days of Patsy McLaughlin. Why, goddamn it, none of the efficiency muckety-mucks in the Main Office ever got a thing on me. They never caught me with my pants down."

"Yes, Willie boy, I know," Walt said mechanically.

"You remember how there wasn't a time you called me for a truck that I didn't pull you out of a hole and come up Johnny-on-the-spot with a truck."

Walt nodded. But he remembered differently. He remembered how difficult Willie used to be to get along with in the old days. But, hell, no use in reminding Willie. Poor Willie Collins was pathetic. God, it was years ago now since the Depression, when Willie was demoted from the Supervision, taken out of Dispatching, and put to driving a tractor under Gas-House McGinty. The two of them had always been at each other's throats. It had been a big joke how every morning McGinty would call Willie up to his tractor board in the Wagon Department, give him a pail, and send Willie out for coffee just to humiliate him. And for a while Casey, who at first had been Collins's clerk, had been Collins's boss. Casey used to send Willie out for coffee, too. Unexpected things happened to a man in life working for a big company like this one.

"It wasn't my fault. It was just that they didn't understand. They didn't know they made a mistake."

"And you were never able to convince them, were you, Willie?"

"Convince the muckety-mucks and big-shots? Of course, I wouldn't have been bumped off my job if Patsy McLaughlin had been the boss. I was old Patsy's ace. But Patsy had already passed away—may the Lord have mercy on his soul. He was the finest man I ever knew, and I ain't ashamed to say that I cried when old Patsy died."

There was a catch in Walt's throat. He recalled how he'd damned near cried himself when he'd heard the news about Patsy's death. Patsy had been like a father to all of them, and working had never been quite the same since Patsy had passed on. Walt felt close to Willie. They had talked and fought on the telephone in the old days. They'd both started on the wagons, and he guessed they were just old teamsters living in this new world of trucks and tractors and airplanes and even air express. Seeing Willie brought back these days of his life that were gone forever. He'd done many of the same things then as he did now. And yet those days seemed better, more interesting, than these. Yes, he'd been younger then, and he'd hoped for lots of things. And Willie, a poor clown, hoping that he'd be promoted back to his old job. But, still, he felt close to Willie. He was sad, sad for the days that were gone and never would come again, and for hopes and dreams that were gone with those days.

"Walt, put in a good word for me with Joe Leonard and Hiram Wolfe. They'll listen to the word of a man like you, Walt. You're an old-timer, you've been in this game for a long time, and they know you know your stuff."

"Well, any time I can do anything for you, Willie, you know I'll do it," Walt said sympathetically.

"You were always white, Walt, you always were a white man."

Walt was embarrassed by Willie's praise. He was both laughing at and feeling sorry for Willie. Hell, he knew, and many others in the Company did, too, that Willie could never get back to his old job. The Company just didn't want Willie dispatching or as a Route Inspector. That was the long and the short of it.

"You know, Walt, I don't gripe. I only say that they made a mistake. So here I am, goddamn it, for over fifteen years, for nearly twenty years, driving a tractor, when I should have been doin' somethin' better. Goddamn it, I was an ace, an ace when I was the Chief Dispatcher up in the Call Department.

Walt wanted to get away from Willie. Hell, this guy Collins would only give him the blues, put him in the dumps. He began to edge away from him to the curb. Willie grabbed his coat and continued:

"Walt, you know, it wasn't fair what they did to

113

me. I know that during the Depression they had to bump some of the Inspectors and Dispatchers. Some of them should have been bumped. They weren't fellows like you and me, with their eyes on the ball, aces. They were just little deuces, that's all. Walt, I tell you, it wasn't fair to do it to me."

Walt nodded. He didn't know what to say to Willie, and Willie was always singing the blues this way every time he could buttonhole anyone to listen to him. Yes, he was sorry for the guy, but what could he do about it? And, hell, who was or who wasn't a Dispatcher didn't seem to make too damned much difference to the Company. He had no illusions about that. They could shove him back on the wagons, just as they had shoved Willie Collins back there in the Depression, and the Company would go right on, and somebody else would do the Dispatching. That was the way it was when a man worked for a living. And he'd been just as happy, he guessed, driving a horse and wagon as he'd been Dispatching. So, what the hell!

"Do you think they'll call me back, Walt?" Willie asked.

"God, I can't say, Willie. But I sure hope they do."

"Have you ate yet, Walt?"

"Yes, I'm just going back to work now."

"I'm feedin'."

Willie shook hands with Walt. They parted. Walt was glad to be shed of Willie Collins. The guy was pathetic.

He wondered what Willie's wife was like. What had Mrs. Collins said to Willie years ago when Willie was bumped from the Supervision? Had she nagged him about it all these years? Did Willie leave a happy home for work every morning? Because if he did, did it matter one snowball in hell if he drove a tractor or if he was in the Supervision?

"Hi, Mr. Callahan," a driver called.

"Hi, Smitty," Walt responded with a smile and a wave of the hand.

Now it was back to the job.

X X X I V

Peg's housework was done. She had nothing more to do but shop. Dorothy had gone. She sat thinking about Dorothy.

—It must be so. It must be so, she told herself in a tense mood.

She decided that it was so. Walt had gone to Dorothy and Joe and talked against her, lied about her, turned them both against her. Dorothy and her brute of a husband were on Walt's side. The way Dorothy had talked proved that. No one would believe it if they hadn't seen it with their own eyes. She wouldn't herself if she hadn't sat looking at her own daughter and listening to her right here in this very parlor only a little while ago. But she knew it was true. Walt had gotten their ear. He must have seen them secretly last week on that night when he'd told her he was playing poker with some of the boys. He had played no poker. He had been over there, talking like an old lady, talking against her.

She rose from her chair and paced the floor, gritting her teeth as she took long strides back and forth. Lying about a mother to a child. Ah, the two of them had always been like that. They had always been too close. When Dorothy was little, they would laugh and joke and have games together, and, fool that she was with her trusting heart, it had never dawned on her that they were laughing at her. How innocent she had been! An innocent mother, raising her family, and what was the father doing but acting like a fiend, turning his six-year-old daughter against her own mother? No wonder Dorothy could only marry a brute like Joe Zarilla. Little wonder!

Now she saw it! Now she knew it! All these years he had been against her! All these years he had been a fiend, and she, so innocent, oh, so innocent. Now the blinders had been taken off her eyes.

Peg paced the house in a mood of rising indignation.

X X X V

When Peg walked into the butcher shop, Marty, the owner, looked away and made a face. His young assistant edged toward the rear so he might escape waiting on her.

"Marty, you're the only honest butcher I know," Peg said.

"Why, thank you, thank you, Mrs. Callahan. I've been in business in this neighborhood for twenty years, and I've always believed that honesty pays."

"If you only knew the robbery that goes on—why isn't something done about it?"

"I don't know. I like to mind my own business and have good relations with my customers. How's Walt, Mrs. Callahan?"

She shook her head sadly.

"He's not feeling too well. Age, you know, Marty, age tells."

"Oh, I'm sorry to hear it. I saw him at Mass two weeks ago, and he was looking in good shape then."

"I have to get him something he can eat. Do you have a capon?"

"Yes, I think I've got just what you want, Mrs. Callahan."

Marty turned and nodded to his assistant to get a capon from the icebox in the rear of the shop.

"Marty, you pick it out yourself. Your young man here is a fine young man, but I want to do business with you. If I have something to say to Father Kenny, I don't go to one of his assistant priests, I go to him. You pick it out for me yourself."

"Yes, I was going to look it over, Mrs. Callahan. I'll get it."

Marty went out to the back of the shop.

Peg turned to the assistant.

"Don't misunderstand me, young man, I mean nothing against you when I ask Marty to give me his personal attention."

"Oh, no, Mrs. Callahan, I understand. There isn't a man in the business who knows and can judge a piece of meat like the boss here."

"I've been coming here to Marty for years." She laughed rather strangely. "He knows better than to sell me a tough cut of meat." Again she laughed strangely. "He once did. Did he ever tell you about the tough cut of sirloin steak he once sold me?"

"No, ma'm, I don't think he did."

"Ha, he'll never forget it," she said, again laughing strangely. "He'll never again sell me steak that's like a piece of rubber."

Marty returned carrying a capon.

"Here's a bird that is going to melt in your old man's mouth, Mrs. Callahan," Marty said to her.

He dropped the capon on the scale.

"Of course, the way I cook meat and fowl, why, you couldn't eat better cooked meat in the best hotels of Chicago."

"I'm sure of it, Mrs. Callahan. As a matter of fact, Walt has commented to me more than once on your cooking when he's been in here buying meat or when I've run into him on the street or at Mass."

"At home, he takes my cooking for granted. Marty, do you take your wife for granted?"

"That's one thing I better not do, Mrs. Callahan," Marty said as he cast a professional eye at the scale.

"I'd forgive you for that, Marty," she said.

"Now, about this capon, Mrs. Callahan," Marty began.

She lost interest and said:

"I'll take it."

X X X V I

How the afternoon had dragged! And during these last hours he'd gotten to feeling more and more pooped out. He'd think of Peg, too, when his mind wasn't on his work, and he'd wonder what her mood would be when he got home—would she be sore, would she nag him, would she be in one of her states? And all he'd done was to drink some beer, too much beer, that was all, and why should she make so goddamn much of it? Hell, when he only did things that other men did he got hell from her, and she sometimes wouldn't let up, and, hell, it wasn't fair to him, it just wasn't fair. And what added to his worry was just the prospect of going home and having Peg sit right on his tail. Now, if he could feel sure he was going home to have some peace and could just pitch into bed and sleep, wake up and eat, and just do nothing but have a peaceful night, then it would be different. But, God, Peg treated him almost like he was a sonofabitch, and, hell, he knew he had his faults, but, after all, how was he a sonofabitch?

It had been a tiring afternoon at work, but now it

was over and he could go home. Go home to what?

Often at the end of his day's work, his mind would be in a kind of fog, and he didn't want to think about anything. When he hit the street, he would feel lost. He would be surprised by the daylight and particularly by the sunshine. That was the way he felt now. He wanted to do something, and he didn't know what he wanted to do. He'd walked down here to Clark and Van Buren almost as if he had been in a trance, and he stood on the corner, blinking his eyes. He wanted something to happen to him which would maybe even change his life. He didn't know what it could be. And he was a little disappointed, because he'd left the Depot and walked here to get his streetcar home, foolishly thinking that something would happen to him and that today would be different from every other day. It was the way he'd felt when he was young, before he'd met Peg, and sometimes even after he had met her and they'd been married. But then, of course, something could have happened. Look at what happened to fat Porky Mulroy. He wondered how Porky was, and what kind of life Porky had had since leaving the Company and his wife.

The noise of traffic drummed in his ears. Funny how the noise back on the Depot platform didn't faze him, but, once out here on the street, it was different, and the noises of the automobiles and trucks and streetcars and the elevated just knocked the thoughts right out of his head. He felt kind of safe and sure of himself at work, and everything seemed more interesting, and he felt he was somebody and was respected by others, and that he was doing his job good enough, but when he left work for the day he had this lost feeling. Now it was just as if he was nobody. And at home he couldn't feel that he was important either, because Peg never gave him credit for anything.

Hell, she ought to give him some credit. Like this afternoon, Mr. Carver, the Superintendent of Terminals, was around, and Mr. Carver called him Walt and told him he always gave full co-operation. Mr. Carver was distant most of the time and did not have much to say to those in the Wagon Department except when he had complaints and criticisms of them about getting freight off the platforms, and most of the Dispatchers bitched about Mr. Carver. But Mr. Carver had praised him and called him Walt, and they'd had a good five-minute chat. There were stories that Mr. Carver was going up in the Company, and there must be something behind them, because Mr. Carver had just about as much as told him so and he'd said, too:

—Walt, you're one man I won't forget.

Hell, some day he might be promoted. That ought to impress Peg. But he didn't know.

Walt's feet still ached. His legs were tired. But he continued to stand on the corner of Clark and Van Buren streets, unable to make up his mind what to do.

He was sure fagged out. His eyelids were heavy, and he knew he could just roll right into sleep. But he didn't want to go home. And, come to think of it, he often felt much the same when he finished work.

And the fine weather, it made him feel down in the mouth. This fine weather just didn't mean much to him at his age. Days like today were made for love. He turned to look at a fine-looking girl who was passing. What a damned inviting piece. But if a man of his age tried to pick her up, she'd think he was a moron. But, God, how he'd like to have something like that, just once more in his life. Peg had been his girl. And it had all turned out so that here he was, standing on this street corner at the age of sixty-three and not wanting to take the streetcar home. And another girl. Thin, but there was enough meat on her. And the legs. Golly, they had shape to them. Peg still had good legs. And the thin girl's face. She was a beauty. Some lucky young fellow would get that girl's beauty.

But, no, it wasn't just a girl, a piece of tail, he wanted. Hell, he could sneak out and go to a whorehouse some night if it was just that. Only he'd look funny at a whorehouse, and suppose he went and couldn't.

Walt became aware of a young fellow, staring at him. He looked down at the sidewalk, abashed. He must be arousing suspicion standing here this way. He felt almost as if this young fellow knew his thoughts. He coughed nervously, not because he had to but because he imagined the young fellow might be thinking him maybe queer, or a moron or something.

Then Walt quickly crossed the street to board a streetcar and go home.

X X X V I I

Sitting next to a window on the car, Walt realized how done in he was. In fact, he was too tired to read his newspaper, as he usually did on the way home. The newspaper usually helped him forget he was going home, and it took his mind away from worrying about the mood Peg might be in. And these last days he had been worrying and thinking and remembering. He didn't know why he was doing this, because, come to think of it, Peg had always been nervous, and she wasn't any different now than she'd been before these last few days. Why did he have it more on his mind now than a month ago or a year ago?

Was something happening to him?

This question, popping into his mind this way, frightened him. He began to sweat under the armpits, and he suddenly felt weak and faint. Christ, was he having a heart attack? His heart began to pound so that he imagined he heard it.

He sat very still in the swaying, bumping car, fearfully expecting the pain of a violent heart attack. Maybe he would die right in the streetcar. Maybe the time had come and his number was being written on the board and he was living his last minutes. He couldn't think. He couldn't pray. He didn't know what to do. He felt far away from the people on the car, as if he were half out of this world, or out of it and all by himself. Was it coming? He couldn't just sit here and wait. But there was nothing he could do.

The car rocked on, jerked to a stop. A few people got off. It started. The stores on the street. People on the street going about their business.

He sighed, telling himself that he didn't want to die.

He couldn't hear his heart any more. The heart attack wasn't coming now. It had been a false alarm, a foolish fear. This was only a result of his hangover and of being tired. But suppose it had been his time? It wouldn't have been so hard to go, so long as he didn't suffer too much pain. Only he hadn't even prayed or said an Act of Contrition, and with the thoughts he'd just been having back there on the corner of Clark and Van Buren. This Saturday he'd go to confession. He ought to go more often from now on. A man of his age never knew when the call would come.

The car swayed, rocked on, and again stopped at a corner.

Hell, everybody had to die some day. He was going to die, and there was no use in his beating his brains out about it. When his time came, he would just grin and bear it and go. Only he didn't want to go ahead of his time, so maybe he ought to go and see Doc Flaherty and get a check-up, and maybe he'd better watch his smoking and the coffee he drank.

Walt slipped down a little in his seat. He'd try and sleep. That would make him forget. Only if he did, he might pass his stop. What would Peg say if he did and came home late? He'd tell her he'd fallen asleep.

Walt closed his eyes.

When he died, what would his wake and funeral be like, and what would be said at the funeral sermon? A good man has lived his time and gone to his Father who is above. A man who worked hard all his life, loved his neighbors and performed his Christian duties, provided for his own, and he leaves his bereaved widow, his children and grandchildren, and he goes to the home of his Father to be judged and to . . . to what?

Walt yawned.

And his wake. Would Peg be in tears, or how would she act when he died? Would she come to see that he wasn't such a bad fellow and . . .

The car rocked along and stopped again. He opened his eyes, unable to fall asleep. Glancing out the window, he told himself that, gee, it was still light and sunny out, and he thought, gosh, if he'd only worked the hours he did now when the kids were young! In those days he used to get home at six, six-thirty, or seven o'clock, often tuckered out from long hours of work, and by the time supper was eaten there hadn't been much time to play with the kids. But now a workingman like Joe, his son-in-law, got home in daylight and didn't work the kind of hours workingmen did years ago. Joe didn't have to work as hard as he'd worked on the wagons. He was glad of that. It was only one of the ways that things had gotten better. And F.D.R. had done it, pretty much, for the workingman. Peg got sore if he praised F.D.R., but he didn't know why—F.D.R. hadn't done her any harm.

He shook his head quizzically. Funny, the things a woman got sore about. Peg got sore, too, if he spoke of her as a grandmother. He liked to think of himself as a grandfather. Of course, it was more understandable, her getting sore about being spoken of as a grandmother than it was about F.D.R. There were many things you could think of to please a woman but they didn't always please her. Like his bringing home that syphon. Often things he thought would please Peg just got her sore.

Hell, going home used to seem better when the kids were young. He couldn't remember too much about the kids, but he was always remembering some little thing. He used to bounce Dorothy on his knees when she was a little tot, or put her on his shoulders and give her horseback rides—he always called them that, but most people called them piggy-back rides—and he used to be Dorothy's horse and get down on his knees, and she would drive him. And he remembered one Sunday morning after church, he had gotten down on his hands and knees with Johnny and Dorothy. He'd pretended that he was a horse, and Johnny was driving him, and Dorothy was Johnny's helper on an express wagon, and Johnny was yelling "giddap" and hitting him with a piece of cord he pretended was a whip, and they rigged up chairs as a wagon, and the kids were getting a big kick out of playing with him. He was having fun and thinking to himself that he was giving the kids a good time, and was doing with them what a father ought to be doing with his kids on a Sunday morning, and then Peg had come in, and, Jesus, how sore she got! God, he couldn't remember all the things she'd said, but she'd said so damned much, screaming and shouting and saying he was spoiling the kids, and laughing at him for letting himself play horse and calling him Horsey Walt.

Walt yawned. He wished the ride were over with. But, then, once it was, he had to get past Peg. He wanted to sleep, and all he hoped was that she wouldn't be all set to nag him and not let him. But sometimes she was different and didn't bother him, and then he could take a nap, and maybe she would be quiet and in a good humor when he got home.

Remembering that Sunday morning so long ago, he still felt that Peg hadn't been fair. She hadn't been fair. And before it had all ended, Dorothy had been crying, and Johnny had been in a corner, kind of cowering, and he and Peg had been standing there in the parlor fighting and yelling and calling each other names and, God, it had just made him want to feel sick, and even remembering it now on the street-car it almost made him feel sick. My God, come to think of it, there'd been so many scenes and quarrels for years, and so many times that he'd come home from work not wanting to and feeling kind of nervous for fear that Peg would be riding on her high horse.

X X X V I I I

Letting himself in by the front door, Walt felt apprehensive. Now maybe he'd have to face the music. But, damn it, he'd gone and done his day's work. She shouldn't criticize him.

"Hello!" he called, trying to sound cheerful.

There was no answer. He made a face. This wasn't a promising sign.

He started toward the back of the apartment. Peg came out of the kitchen.

"Oh, I didn't hear you come in."

"I called as I came in."

"I didn't hear you."

"Well, how are you, Peg?"

"Oh, I'm tired. I had to clean the house and shop, and I'm cooking you a supper with everything you like. I thought you'd need a good meal."

"Gee, thanks, Peg," he said, drawing her to him and kissing her cheek.

She was unresponsive.

"I bought a capon. I picked it out myself."

"I know it's going to be good, Peg."

He was grateful to her for not being belligerent.

"I'm tired. I'm going to take a nap."

"Don't get on the bed in your dirty work clothes. I can't wash sheets all the time, and the laundries are getting dearer every day, and I haven't found one yet that doesn't lose things or ruin what they do send back."

"I won't, Peg," he said.

He quickly went to the bedroom, took off his clothes, and dropped onto the bed. He didn't have to worry about anything. He could sleep until supper-time.

X X X I X

His hour or so of sleep had been so sweet. Yes, sweet. And then he'd taken a hot bath, put on clean clothes, and now it was just as if he hadn't drunk all that beer and had a hangover today. He was tired, but it was a kind of pleasant tiredness. He had on clean under-wear, clean socks, a freshly pressed pair of pants, and a clean white shirt. He left it open at the collar. And he was shaved. He felt pretty good. And he felt healthy. That scare on the streetcar had only been a foolish worry. Maybe his time was still far off. After all, if he wasn't healthy, and if he wasn't in fair shape, and if his old ticker wasn't ticking in pretty good order, why, then, he wouldn't have been able to get through the day as well as he had, would he? But he just wanted to forget last night. After all, all he'd done was to drink too much beer.

The smell of food seemed to whet his appetite. And there was the bird, nicely cooked, and the potatoes, the salad, the bowl of gravy. It was a real spread, and he was grateful to Peg for it, and for having gone to all this trouble for him.

"Gee, this is swell, Peg," he said, gazing at the table and sniffing.

"I hope you appreciate it and realize how hard it was getting this supper ready for you."

"I do, I do, Peg," he said earnestly.

"The food's getting cold. Carve the capon before your meal is cold. After all the work I did cooking it for you, do you want a cold meal?"

"It won't get cold," he said.

He picked up the carving knife and fork. He liked to carve and was proud of how well he usually did it, but Peg never gave him credit for his skill. He began to cut up the capon neatly and with a feeling of real pleasure.

"Can't you carve any faster than that? I don't want to eat a cold meal," Peg said curtly.

"A man can't look at a fowl and have it carved. I'm carving."

"Don't carve too much."

"I won't," Walt said, sinking the knife in beside the left leg.

"It's always the same—I try my hardest to fix you a nice dinner and to have everything on the table warm, and then it gets cold. You don't even care. Dorothy is just the same. She doesn't care if she serves warm or cold food."

"It won't be cold. Go ahead and serve, and I'll have the bird carved in a jiffy."

In a moment he looked up with pride and said:

"There, it's all done, and the food isn't cold."

"It would be if I hadn't made you hurry. You'd still be carving."

X L

"You might tell me you like the supper I cooked you," she said.

Walt was eating with real appetite. He looked up, and then, when he'd swallowed what he'd been chewing, he said, smiling:

"I do. I like it."

"You wouldn't have told me if I hadn't asked."

"But, Peg, I did tell you. I told you I liked it at least four times."

"You didn't. You did not."

He knew he'd praised her, and he couldn't understand why she should deny such a simple fact.

"Do you like the dressing?"

"I sure do. I've been stuffing myself with it, I like it so much . . . Peg, you're a dandy cook—and a fine wife."

She gazed stonily down at her own plate, picked up her fork, and went on eating.

X L I

Watching Walt eat with gusto, Peg kept thinking that he swallowed his food like a pig. He was so disgusting at the table that it was hard, very hard, a trial and a tribulation, for her to have to eat with him. He wasn't a man because he wasn't a human being. He was an animal. How could a woman eat when, night after night, she had to sit at the table opposite an animal like him.

Just look at him slobber!

Oh, she was deserving of pity. There was nothing, just nothing she could do, because here she was, living with a pig and a horse, an animal who looked like a human being and a man but who couldn't be called a human being or a man, and there was no use, no use whatever, in even telling him how she felt. He couldn't understand.

There was a morose expression on her face. She ate slowly. Now and then she glanced up from her plate to see him pushing food into his mouth. She saw how satisfied he was, and thought that his face just looked stupid. Why, it was almost enough to make her want to scream, to get up and run out of the house and go away and never see him again, to make her want to rush to the bathroom and chuck up her food.

And she sweated over a hot stove to cook this meal for him. She had gone out to buy the food, full of the best intentions. The care and love and thought she had given to picking out the capon at Marty's. And before doing this she had cleaned the house, getting down on her hands and knees and scrubbing the bathroom floor. And what for? For him to come home and eat like an animal?

"Peg, if some of them fellows down at the Express Company knew how good a cook my wife was, they'd just look at me green with envy, green-eyed with envy," Walt said sincerely.

"Are you finished?" she asked coldly.

"Yeh, just about," he answered, somewhat disappointed that she didn't react to his praise.

"And it was a damned swell dinner, Peg."

"It could have been better. I put too much sage in the dressing."

"Oh, I liked it just as it was."

"I'm glad that at last I cooked something you liked."

"I always liked your cooking, Peg."

Now she seemed in a better mood. She went on eating, finishing what was on her plate.

He sat back, contented and full. He would have his coffee, and he would fall asleep over his newspaper, and then, a little later, he would go to bed, get himself a good long night's sleep, and he'd be feeling tiptop in the morning. But should he tonight?

After all, he was still a man, and, goddamn it, he was proud to think that the old juices weren't dried up in him yet. He tried to observe Peg carefully without making her aware of it. God, he and Peg had been doing it for years and years, almost thirty years now. How many times had they?

"If you've finished, I'll get you your coffee. And I bought apple pie. I was going to bake a pie, but I just couldn't with the shopping and the housework I have to do, getting down on my knees and scrubbing floors, and you'll just have to put up with the pie I bought at Condon's Bakery."

"That's perfectly okay, Peg," he said. "This supper has been one of the best you ever cooked, and that's saying a mouthful. But it isn't as much of a mouthful as the supper was," he said, laughing at his pun.

"I hope that syphon works. I put some cream in it."

"Oh, it'll work, all right."

"How do you know it will?"

"I just do."

"It didn't work for you." She pointed to the wall on her right. "The wall is still stained from the last time you used it."

"That was an accident, Peg. I must have just pressed too hard. It worked for you."

"Yes, I worked it," she said triumphantly.

She got up, picked up both their plates, and went to the kitchen.

He had been on the verge of telling her that he thought he had better skip dessert because he was so full, but he decided he'd better not, since she had gotten him the pie and had made whipped cream. He hoped the syphon worked. Apple pie was one of his favorites. She might get antagonistic if he didn't have dessert now. And he didn't want tonight spoiled, especially after this supper. He tapped his knuckles lightly on the table; they'd gotten through supper so far without any fighting.

"It'll take another minute for the coffee to percolate. When you make coffee in the morning, it's too weak. I have to make fresh coffee for myself every morning."

"I'll try to let it perk longer in the mornin', Peg. I guess I get too impatient. I'm sorry."

Peg started clearing away more dishes. He half rose and said:

"Let me help you, Peg."

"You wouldn't know where to put them, you'd make me twice as much work."

He sat back in his chair. He'd rather sit here than clear the dishes, and, then, he'd done his day's work and worked as hard as Peg. He'd worked as hard or harder in his life than she had here in the house. A man who worked and provided had a right to sit back and wait for his coffee and let his meal digest and let his wife clear away the dishes and wash them. That was division of labor.

Hell, he told himself, he wasn't asking too much just to sit here in peace, have his coffee, and feel . . . well, feel relaxed and content and not to have little things bothering him and weighing on his mind.

X L I I

"Say, that looks swell," Walt said when Peg carried in a tray with the cups of coffee and pieces of apple pie with whipped cream on them.

"It's the best I could do," she answered, setting down the tray and serving the coffee and pie.

"It's good enough for me. And say . . ." His voice became enthusiastic. "Say, the syphon worked, didn't it?"

"I made it work. Look at me!"

He gazed across the table at her, puzzled.

"Did I squirt any whipped cream in my eyes or on my hair and my face?"

"Why, no," he said seriously.

Then he felt foolish. Was she pulling his leg or was she trying to fight with him?

"I squirted it carefully. Before you use it again, I'll give you a lesson on how to make it squirt."

"Oh, I know how to use it now, Peg."

"Well, if you want to squirt whipped cream and root beer all over the walls and the floor—you're the man of the house, not me."

"Peg, I only meant—"

"Go ahead, eat your pie and drink your coffee before it gets cold."

He gave her a hangdog look and then he resolutely set to eating his pie. He had to get it eaten, or she might go off the handle. And he didn't want that to happen. Hell, he hoped he didn't belch or that his stomach didn't make noises, because she could hear it and might call it to his attention or make fun of him.

They were both silent for several moments. The silence made him uneasy. He felt a need to talk.

"Oh, I almost forgot to tell you, Peg."

"You never tell me much anyway."

"There's never a lot to tell, and sometimes when I do try to tell you about some incident that happened at the Depot, or something funny that someone said, you don't always seem to want to listen to me."

"I always listen. You don't listen to me."

He wanted to tell her of how, five or six nights ago, he'd begun to tell a story about Mr. Tuttle but she hadn't listened. He checked himself. No use reminding her that she had been in the wrong.

"Well, what's the story you were going to tell me?" she asked rather curtly.

"Oh," he exclaimed.

He struggled to remember what it was he'd wanted to tell her and became uneasy about it.

"Is it so important that you can't even remember it? Maybe you should tie another piece of string on your finger."

"I saw Mr. Carver today."

"Who's he?"

"He's Superintendent of Terminals."

"You saw the Superintendent of Terminals? You work in a terminal and you see the Superintendent of Terminals?" she commented scornfully.

"I didn't tell you yet."

"Well, I've been waiting for ten minutes for you to tell me. It better be something good."

"But you wouldn't let me tell you, Peg."

"I suppose I held a knife over you and told you I'd kill you if you told me about Mr. Carver, the Superintendent of Wagons."

"It's Mr. Carver, and he's Superintendent of Terminals, not wagons."

"Well, then, terminals."

"No, you interrupted me."

"I interrupted you—when I've been sitting here just waiting for you to tell me whatever it is you're trying to tell me?"

"It might be important—for both of us."

"Then, for God's sake, tell me what it is."

"Well, he called me Walt, for one thing."

"Is that what you took so much time to tell me?"

"He doesn't call any other fellow in the Supervision or the Wagon Department by their first name."

"So he calls you Walt," she said.

"It's not just that he called me Walt. That's—that's like, well, it's like a symptom."

"Can't you get to the point of whatever it is you are trying to tell me?"

"That's what I'm trying to do. He was friendly and stopped to talk with me for about five minutes."

"I thought you worked so hard you didn't have time for talk."

"Well, he's an important man in the Company, and there are stories going around that he's going up the ladder, and that's the point of what I'm trying to tell you—"

"Well, tell it to me then," she interrupted.

"I am, if you'll let me."

"You've been talking until my coffee got cold and you haven't told me the story yet," she said with an ironical laugh.

"Well, he said he wouldn't forget me. That means maybe if he does go up, well, some day he'll promote me."

"He better hurry up. You're sixty-three already."

"I don't have to go on my pension until I'm seventy."

"And so if you don't grow too old too soon, you might be promoted."

Walt silently finished his pie and coffee. He was too deeply wounded to speak.

X L I I I

Walt shook his head sleepily from side to side and blinked his eyes, and then he let out a big, noisy yawn.

He was glad Peg had told him not to bother about helping her do the dishes. But she couldn't say he hadn't offered to help, because he had.

He picked up the newspaper, looked at it, held it in his hand, but he just didn't have the energy or the interest to read it. He heard his stomach making rolling, digestive noises, and he belched. He was glad Peg wasn't in the room to hear. He patted his stomach. He had something of a paunch, not too much, but something. But then, hell, look at Casey. Casey was younger than he was, a damned sight younger than he was.

His stomach had stopped making noises now. He slumped slightly in his chair. He let out another yawn. He felt kind of peaceful at last.

And that conversation today with Mr. Carver. Suppose Mr. Carver became General Manager and should make him an Assistant Superintendent. Hell, he could do the job. He knew the game well enough now after all these years. He'd gone on the wagons as a helper when he'd only been a kid of seventeen. Next year would make it fifty years in the express business. Almost half a century of work—now, that was a record to be proud of and it ought to be appreciated. And he could handle a bigger job. He knew he could. Golly, he could just see himself as an Assistant Super, coming around to his old Depot, seeing that goddamned cantankerous foreman, Mr. Tuttle. And having a desk and sitting there and dictating letters. How would he be at that? He hardly wrote ten letters a year, but as an Assistant Super he'd have to dictate letters, and he didn't know how good he'd be at that. But that wouldn't be any obstacle. And maybe he'd come up with a lot of ideas to make things run better, only he wouldn't go in none for this damned efficiency that only made paper work and got men sore. He could see himself going around to his Depots in a car, checking up and knowing he was liked. Hell, plenty of fellows would be glad if he did become an Assistant Super, and they'd sincerely congratulate him. And, then, the money. Four-ninety a month. He'd get one hundred and fifty dollars more a month, and with that he could get a house for Peg and himself. They should have bought one years ago, and if they had, it would be all paid for now. Heinie Mueller owned his own house, and, besides saving money, he got a lot of pleasure out of it. But Peg had been dead set against it. Funny, but she was always dead set against anything new or a change. She'd even been against that syphon.

Then, too, his pension would be bigger if he became an Assistant Super, and he could really live on it when he retired and not have to take another job.

But maybe he was only daydreaming; maybe Mr. Carver would forget all about him or not become General Manager. Still, why couldn't he be an Assistant Super?

He sank lower in his chair and yawned again. From the kitchen he heard Peg washing the dishes. He was waiting for her to finish and come in, hoping she wouldn't be hostile or antagonistic.

He nodded his head and continued to sit in a kind of pleasant and soothing stupor.

X L I V

Peg had said something, but he hadn't quite heard her right away, because he was just sitting here, just sitting almost as if he was away outside of the world and was someplace else, off all by himself.

Then he looked across the parlor at Peg.

"I don't mind it, dear," she said in an icily sweet voice.

"Oh, dear, I was half asleep."

"You always act this way and don't pay much attention to me, but I'm used to it. I only asked if you enjoyed your dinner."

"Yes, Peg, I did. Very much. It was a swell meal."

He sank back a little in his chair. He didn't want to talk now. He couldn't think of anything to say. God, even if he were with an assemblage of the big shots of the Company now, he couldn't get up any interest. That was the way he felt.

But he felt that he had to say something to Peg. She wanted to talk, and if he didn't talk with her and show some interest, she'd get sore. He knew that it got lonely enough for her, and she didn't have anybody to talk to all day, and he knew that at night a man and his wife who were alone together and getting old should talk to each other and be sociable, but, God, what could he talk about right now? It was just as if there wasn't any talk in him. He felt that way. Tired-like. Peaceful and tired-like. If they could just sit here, and each of them think and remember and have their own thoughts, and know they were together, and not have to say anything . . . if they could be like that. But they couldn't. Because that wasn't the way it was. And, my God, after all these years, he still didn't know how to talk to her so as not to get her dander up.

"You're tired?" Peg asked.

"Yes, I am. I'm kind of sleepy. I thought I would just sit here a while and think and maybe look at my paper and turn in and hit the hay early."

"Let me get you a glass of beer. It will relax you and make you sleep better."

"No, no, thanks, Peg, I don't think I ought to drink any beer."

"Well, I'll get it for you to relax you."

"Gosh, I'm relaxed," Walt said.

Peg was sitting on the edge of her chair, tapping her feet on the rug, moving her knees, changing her position in little ways, clasping and unclasping her hands, looking down at her hands and legs, glancing at him and all around the room. She seemed mighty nervous and jittery to him. It was she, not he, who wasn't relaxed.

"Well, I offered to get it for you. I try to take care of you and do for you the things a wife ought to do."

"Yes, I know you do. And, Peg, I do appreciate it, and I appreciate the feed you put on for me tonight. It was tops. Tops."

"Dorothy said I don't take good enough care of you."

His eyes opened wide. He sat up.

"When did she say that?"

"Today."

"What did she do, phone you? How are she and Joe and the kids?"

"I told you she was here to see me."

"No, you didn't."

"It just goes to show you. I told you she was here, but you just never listen to me."

But she hadn't told him. He'd remember it if she had.

"It doesn't matter. Even if it was something important I told you, it would be the same—you wouldn't hear me," Peg said disconsolately.

"But you didn't tell me, dear. How is Dorothy?"

"I never expected the day would come when you would lie to my face, Walt Callahan."

Walt opened his mouth to speak, but he didn't. What the hell difference did it make if she had or hadn't told him? It wasn't worth fighting and quarreling about.

"I'm sorry, dear. I guess I just wasn't listening, or I must have forgotten that you told me Dorothy was over to see you today."

"She talked as if you might have been talking to her against me, complaining against me and running me down. I never ran you down in the eyes of your own children."

"But, Peg, I ain't talked to Dorothy since that night she telephoned. Remember, Peg? You heard everything I said. It was the night I brought home the Little Gem Syphon. And, Peg, why should I want to talk against you to Dorothy?"

"I don't know," she said dully. "But it doesn't matter."

"Honest, Peg . . ." he began.

But he didn't go on, because she looked as if she wasn't listening.

They both sat silent now. Walt could see that she was very sad and depressed. And when she was like this, it got him, too. He was beginning to feel almost as if it were his fault that Peg felt this way.

But what had he done to her?

"Are you sure you don't want a glass of beer to relax your nerves?"

He was tempted. Maybe it would make him feel better and less gloomy. But, no, he wouldn't. He'd drunk enough beer last night.

"Thanks, dear, not tonight."

"Don't say I didn't offer to get it for you, and don't go telephoning Dorothy complaining that I don't take care of you and wait on you hand and foot."

"But, dear, I never did that."

She said nothing more. She seemed very much on edge now, and the two of them sat in gloomy silence.

X L V

In his dream he'd heard loud voices and noises, and then there had been a huge lion that looked as much like a cat as it did like a lion, and it had been coming at him, roaring, and then, just as he was afraid, terribly afraid, he'd waked up, and found that Peg had turned on the electric light and had really waked him up shouting at him. He was bewildered.

"Is anything the matter, Peg?" he asked, blinking his eyes because of the light.

She was standing near the bed in her underwear. The look on her face was enough to give a man the creeps.

"He asks me if anything is the matter?" she proclaimed in a loud, rasping voice.

"Well, is there?"

"If there was, could I depend on you? Could I count on you? It's a good thing for me that there isn't anything the matter."

"Then what the hell did you wake me up for?"

"As if you didn't wake me up last night, snoring like a bull and wallowing all over the bed."

"I didn't know what I was doing, and I didn't wake you up on purpose," he countered.

"That's it, scream at me, shout! Bully me at all hours of the day and night, just as if I was a dirty, low-down chauffeur working for you."

"But you're doing the shouting and screaming, not me."

"Abuse me! Lie about me! You're in a foaming rage. You're glaring at me and foaming out of the mouth like a man from the booby hatch, the booby hatch, the booby hatch, the booby hatch."

"What the hell are you talkin' about?"

"What am I talking about? Tomorrow morning, go to work and tell the expressmen that your wife picks on you—you, a big hulk of a man—picked on."

"Peg, I want to go to sleep."

"Who's stopping you?"

"You are. You woke me up, and you won't stop talkin' and shoutin' at me and fightin' with me. I don't want to fight with you. I want to sleep. I got to get up early in the mornin' and go to work. You know that."

"You're keeping me awake. Everybody in the block can hear you shouting insults at me. You might just as well beat me, beat me to a pulp, as to do what you're doing to me."

He clenched his fist under the blanket, but then he immediately unclenched it. God, was he nuts? She was shouting and screaming. She was fighting and she was denying that she had waked him. God, he couldn't understand Peg. He couldn't understand women.

He turned his head away from her and said:

"I'm goin' to sleep. Good night."

"Oh, that God would only see your cruelty," she declaimed in a throbbing, disturbed voice.

Walt determined not to answer her. He remembered that she had done things like this to him before. Yes, sometimes she just got into some kind of a goddamn state like this and just kept on going and wouldn't stop.

"He wounds me in the heart. He pierces me in the heart, and he might as well shoot an arrow or stick a knife into my heart, and then he sleeps in peace. Oh, God, that I am married to such a man! Oh, God, that such a man can live!" she declaimed, her voice still throbbing and disturbed.

Maybe if he counted sheep he wouldn't hear her and could go to sleep. One, two, three. . . . One sheep . . . two sheep . . . three sheep. . . . Baa, baa, little black sheep . . . one . . . one sheep, two sheep, three sheep . . . four sheep . . .

"How could I have known I was marrying a man without a heart?"

No, he couldn't count sheep. He couldn't keep his mind on it. He was tired. If he didn't get his sleep, he'd be all done in in the morning. Couldn't he shut her up?

But now she was quiet. Maybe the storm was over. He'd pretend he was asleep. He almost snored. But she might start up again criticizing him for snoring, and that would get under his skin. No, he would just lie quiet and pretend to sleep.

For a moment it was quiet. He wanted to sigh with relief, but he restrained himself and tried to be as still as he possibly could. He wanted her to think he was sound asleep. He was aware of his own breathing. It seemed to him that he was breathing very loudly.

He decided that Peg had toned down and that she'd come to bed and go to sleep. Now all he had to do was to get to sleep himself. Hell, he felt that never in his whole life had he wanted to sleep as much as he did now. He began to doze off.

Suddenly there was a loud banging of a dresser drawer. He sat up with a start.

"Goddamn you, what the hell are you doing?"

She turned on him and gave him a look he never could remember having seen on her face before. She slowly came closer to the bed, with that look on her face, her eyes kind of shining and staring straight at him almost as if they were burning into him, and her lips pressed together. And as she came closer, her face was damp and perspiring, and her hair was mussed up and wild-looking.

He was afraid. Never, as long as they had been married, had she seemed or looked like this. He waited, all jittery inside. She stood over the bed a moment. Then, in a voice that wasn't at all like her usual one, but was flat, she said to him:

"Don't fight me. Kiss me."

She bent down.

He kissed her damp cheek. He was shaky.

She turned away, and with her back to him began to take off her underwear. He dropped his head back on the pillow and his shoulders sagged, and, still afraid, not knowing exactly how he was feeling, and thinking he kind of felt as if he had just had a narrow escape from being run over and killed by an automobile, he lay back and watched her put on her nightgown over her thin body.

But she turned out the light and quietly got into bed. Then in a meek, low voice, she said:

"Good night, Walt."

"Good night, Peg."

X L V I

With her kimono open, Peg sat in Walt's chair in the darkened parlor and stared at the night through the window. She couldn't sleep. Just as she'd been going off, he'd begun to snore. His loud snores had waked her, and now here she was, all alone in the night, waiting for the morning, waiting for him to get out of the house.

Oh, would the morning never come?

She wanted to see it light out. She wanted to see

the sunshine. There was no sunshine in her heart. There had never, never been sunshine in her life.

There he was, snoring again.

No man on earth, no man could make as much noise in his sleep and snore like Walt Callahan. But he had never been a man. He was old and gray and ugly, and she would have to take care of him as he got sick and weak. It was ugly, just ugly to think of it. And he was ugly. And he had done everything he could to make her life ugly.

Fool, innocent fool that she was, she had thought he would give her comfort and understanding. That was why she had given herself to him, to get comfort. He'd been big and handsome, and he had looked strong, and her mother had just drummed it into her, day and night, day and night, that she had to get married. Her mother's words had beat in her head, beat, beat like . . . like what? Like Walt Callahan's snores.

There he was, snoring again. You could hear him snore in every room, every corner of the house. God, she'd bet even the neighbors could hear him snore, the way the neighbors had used to hear her mother screaming at her and shouting and nagging, telling her to get married.

Her mother had wanted to get rid of her. And her father?

Peg cried softly. Her mother had killed her father. It was because of her mother that he'd drunk. Nothing had stopped her mother, and now, now she could understand how her father had been driven to drink, and how he never would have had that accident and died if her mother had not driven him to it.

Oh, would the morning never come?

There he was, snoring away. Some day she would go out of her mind because of him and his snoring. If she had to go on like this night after night, not able to sleep because of him, she could . . . she could . . .

A terrible fear contorted her, and she curled up on the chair and trembled. And she remembered how one night as a little girl she couldn't sleep, and she had been afraid and gotten out of bed and run toward her mother's bedroom. The door was open. She'd heard them and seen them in the darkness. She hadn't known what her parents were doing and she'd thought her father was beating her mother. She'd run back to bed, trembling and whimpering. And she'd felt all alone, alone and unloved and afraid. She'd wanted to die. She'd been afraid she would die, and she'd wanted to die, and she'd been too afraid to cry for fear they'd hear her and that her father would come in and hurt her. And she'd heard him coming, his heavy walk. Step by step, and he'd come into the bedroom. She had lain perfectly still and pretended to be asleep. And when he'd bent down she'd smelled the whisky and tobacco on his breath, and he'd talked to her and asked her if she was awake. But she hadn't stirred. He'd touched her, and it had been like ice and like death touching her. Oh, it had been awful.

And he'd gone back to her mother, but she had not slept but had just lain quiet, quiet as a mouse. And their loud breathing, and her mother asking her father to hurt her. Yes, she'd heard that, too. And at last on that awful night she'd heard her father snoring, and she, an innocent little girl, she had just lain awake, quiet as a mouse, so afraid, and just waiting for the night to end.

Oh, wouldn't the morning ever come?

There he was, snoring again.

Peg went to the window and gazed at the dark street. She turned and went softly on bare feet to the bedroom. She stood looking down at her sleeping husband in the darkness.

He was snoring away.

She didn't know why she didn't scream. She didn't know why she didn't do something. She stood like one frozen.

He snored again.

She went to the kitchen and poured herself a large glass of milk.

X L V I I

She could hear his snores even out here in the kitchen. Was there no escape for her?

Peg gulped down a glass of milk. She sat with her

arms lying limply on the kitchen table. All sorts of thoughts were spinning around in her head. Oh, sometimes her thoughts cut to her heart just as if she had been cut with a knife.

—Oh, the tears in my heart, she tragically told herself.

She was getting old. This was the way her life was ending. This! This was what had become of her.

—Oh, God, wouldn't that snoring ever stop? Stop! Stop!

—You'll never be any good.

How often her mother had said that to her.

She jerked her head in surprise and fear. It had seemed almost as if she'd heard her mother's voice again.

—You'll never be any good. Marry him or you'll become a streetwalker.

Her mother had told her that, too, told her to marry Walt or she'd be a whore. Oh, if she'd been a whore, her life would have been better than it was, better than this.

Her mother's words came back as if she were hearing them now, as if her mother were right here in the kitchen with her. Her mother had cursed her and ignored her and sometimes beat her, and once had even locked her in a closet for hours, yes, for hours, and she could remember being alone in the dark, screaming and beating her poor little fists against the door and crying and being so afraid. Oh, what had she done? Why had her mother hated her and told her she was no good. And Walt hated her. He hated her as much as her mother had. And was her mother watching from beyond the grave, hating her, watching her from Hell and coming up from the fires of Hell to tell her all over again?

—I hate you!

—You're no good!

—I hate you!

—Marry him or be a whore, you whore!

She seemed to hear the very words, and, with her lips trembling, she looked around the kitchen to see in what corner her dead mother, up from the fires of Hell, might be lurking and staring at her, staring with eyes burning like the coals of Hell and the devil-burning eyes of hatred.

Her hand shook.

Her nerves!

She pressed her hands hard against her temples.

Oh, she had to pull herself together. She had to get it out of her mind that her mother was watching her and hating her from the other side of the grave, from Hell itself.

She had always been a good girl. She had.

She had done nothing. She had tried, oh, tried to be a good wife and a good mother, and she had grown old doing it, and for what? For this kind of life? Asking herself this question, she made a sweeping gesture with her hands. For Walt Callahan, who hated her in this world the way her mother hated her in eternity.

—Dry tears!

She liked those two words. She was shedding dry tears every minute of her life.

She poured another glass of milk and drank it slowly. It was soothing to drink milk. It made her feel a little better. But not in her heart, her wounded heart. Because her poor heart was cut and wounded.

She sighed, lit a cigarette, and puffed nervously. She asked herself who cared about her. Who even knew what she really was, or what her life had been, or what her side of her marriage with Walt had really been like? Who knew how Walt Callahan had failed her when he could have saved her? Who knew what he had done to her, to her life? He had taken her that night in her home, but he had not saved her, and now, every minute of the day and night, he hated her. His hatred of her was killing her. Killing her soul.

Peg got up and slowly went back to the parlor. She sank listlessly into Walt's chair. She wanted the light on, but she didn't have the energy to go and turn it on.

She would sit here and wait for the morning, the sunshine, the dawn, the light. Birds singing in the sunshine. Birds singing and flying away, singing in the sunshine.

Peg sighed. Her shoulders sagged. She fixed rigid eyes on the darkness in the parlor. Her lips moved. She said nothing.

Then she heard Walt snoring again.

—Would that old devil never stop it?

She slumped farther in her chair.

"The hearts of birds. Singing. Sunshine," she mumbled softly.

Suddenly she got up and walked very slowly to the bedroom. She got into bed and curled up closely against Walt.

He snored and turned over toward the wall in his sleep.

X L V I I I

"Why, Peg, you didn't have to get up and cook my breakfast," Walt said, surprised at finding her by the stove.

"I was awake. I didn't sleep much last night, I didn't sleep until dawn," she said, turning toward him.

For a moment she seemed almost unrecognizable. She looked wretched and miserable. Her eyes were dull. Her face and neck seemed scrawny. Her hair was disheveled. There were circles under her eyes. And her voice. She had spoken with such meekness. Then he noticed that her hands were trembling slightly.

"Peg, you go back to bed and get a good rest," Walt said gently.

"No," she said with a quiver in her voice. "I'll cook your breakfast."

"But, Peg, I can do it, and you look like you need more rest."

"I can cook your breakfast," she repeated, speaking as though she had to struggle to think of every word.

Walt sat down and waited, but he wished she'd go back to bed. She was acting queerly, and she didn't seem well.

"Peg, are you all right? You're not sick, are you?"

"No," she said listlessly.

He watched her closely as she bent over the stove. God, she was so thin. He felt sorry, so sorry for her, seeing her this way. Was there anything wrong with her?

"You're sure you're all right?"

"Yes," she said.

She sounded as if she would burst into tears at any moment.

"I'm always all right," she said with self-pity.

Walt shook his head from side to side, feeling helpless. Glum and worried, he sat waiting.

She set bacon and eggs and coffee and toast at his place.

"I hope you like your breakfast."

"It looks fine."

Bringing in a cup of black coffee for herself, she sat down opposite him. Walt ate, but without appetite.

She sighed, and he looked up anxiously.

"Anything the matter, Peg?"

"No . . . nothing, nothing's the matter."

Her voice was so strange and sad.

"Are you sure? You don't need a doctor, do you? Do you want me to stay home from work and take care of you?"

"I'm all right," she said, speaking slowly and in that same, strange tone of voice.

"Because if there's anything you want me to do, please tell me and I'll do it."

She didn't answer, but looked into her coffee cup.

"I'm all right . . . all right," she said in the same way she had a moment ago.

Walt kept quiet because he felt that if he spoke, he might rock the boat. Peg sat drinking her coffee and staring past him with a look of utter dejection.

2

Walt was happy to be at the family gathering in his son Jack's house, seeing his kids and grandkids. He liked Maggie, Jack's wife, and Joe, his son-in-law. He'd looked forward to this day all week. And it was good not to have to spend the Sunday alone with Peg. It was getting harder and harder for him to have any peace of mind when he was alone with her. And much as he wanted to get away and go out without her, he was kind of afraid of doing it because she asked so many questions and kept tripping him up even though there was really nothing to be tripped up over. But somehow, because of the way she went at him, she would confuse him, and then she would manage to trip him up. And she would get the idea that things happened differently from the way they really did. She'd get her own idea of what happened, and she would believe that, even though the truth was completely different. Just being in the same room with Peg now made him damned nervous, so that he wasn't sure of what he ought to say. When he started to talk, he would think of what she might think of what he was saying, and this made him extra careful, because he didn't know how she'd take it.

"Father, have some more beer," Dorothy said.

"Yes, do," Maggie urged.

Maggie was small, dark, and thin, and Walt believed Jack was very happy with her. This made him feel good.

"Yeh," Jack was saying. "Yeh, we're gettin' our new car. Next week."

"Father, didn't you ever want a car?" Dorothy asked.

Walt hesitated. He'd wanted to own an automobile for a number of years now, just as he'd wanted his own home. But it was Peg. He didn't want to tell Dorothy and his son, or his son-in-law and his daughter-in-law, that his wife wouldn't let him get an automobile.

"I wouldn't trust myself in a car with your father," Peg volunteered.

"Oh, Father can drive, can't you, Father?" Dorothy asked.

"He can't even remember where he puts his shoes at night. For all I know, he would want the car to go forward, and, the first thing you know, it would be going backward," Peg said.

Walt felt humiliated. And he noticed that his son-in-law, Joe, was looking at Peg with a queer expression on his face.

"I wouldn't want to be killed in an automobile accident," Peg said.

"You're not afraid of riding in cars, are you?" Joe asked Peg.

"Goodness, no, not with a good driver. Not with my son John driving."

"Jack, you got something your old man hasn't got," Joe said lightly.

Peg glared at Joe but said nothing. He laughed good-naturedly.

"I don't imagine I'd get any pleasure out of driving a car," Walt said.

"But the things you can do and the places you can go! Why, last year my girl friend and her husband, that's Mary and Pete, they went to California on their vacation and had a grand time. They saw the Grand Canyon, the desert, the Pacific Ocean, and they had a wonderful time," Maggie said.

"Yes, we've gotten about and seen a bit of the country in our old jalopy," Jack said.

"If you had a car, Father, you and Mother could take some trips," Dorothy said, looking at Walt.

Walt nodded his head, and he got to thinking of how little he had seen of the country. When the kids were young, they weren't able to go away on vacations. But, still, Jack and Dorothy went away with their families on vacations. Times had changed that way. During these last years he'd wanted to go somewhere on his vacations, but Peg never would. And, heck, with an automobile, they could. Almost everybody seemed to have one, and sometimes at work he was kidded and told he was too cheap to buy a car. He thought, too, of how Peg and he might have done many more things than they had, and that they ought to have gotten much more fun out of life. Certainly his children seemed to be enjoying life more than he and Peg had. He was sincerely glad about this, but, even so, it made him kind of sad.

Jack and Joe were talking about their bowling now and kidding each other. Joe asked Walt if he bowled any more.

"You used to be a good bowler, Walt," Joe said.

"Oh, I don't know. I just haven't played much in the last few years."

"Jack here is a better bowler than his father ever was," Peg said.

Joe ignored Peg and turned to Walt.

"Yes, Walt, you were good enough for me to wish you were on my team."

"I'm gettin' too old for bowling, I guess," Walt said apologetically.

"What the hell you doin', Walt, kiddin' yourself?" Joe asked.

Walt grinned rather sheepishly.

"I remember, Dad, how I used to watch you bowl. You were pretty good," Jack said.

"Listen, he's still good enough to beat you for my money," Joe told Jack.

"You might be right. God, I remember when I was about eighteen, Dad—remember, you took me along one night and you bowled one-sixty, one seventy-three, and then two-o-four? I was proud of you, I was."

Walt beamed. He looked gratefully at Jack, and

there was a flooding feeling of affection for his son. He remembered the ball games he'd taken Jack to as a boy. Gosh, Peg had even crabbed about that. He'd had good times like that with Jack. He became nostalgic for the days when Jack and Dorothy were young. He guessed maybe those were the best days of his life. He looked at his children tenderly. It was hard to think they had once been little tots and that he'd carried them on his back. God, it was a mystery the way kids grew into men and women, it was.

"Ever see any more ball games, Dad?" Jack asked.

"No, I haven't seen a game in two-three years. I guess I kind of lost interest, Jack."

"I'll have to come over and get you in the new car one of these Sundays, and we'll drive out to the ball game and it'll be just like old times, Dad."

"Let's," Walt said gratefully.

"You can ring me in on your jaunt," Joe said.

"Fine, we'll all three go," Walt said.

"The men of the family," Dorothy said proudly.

Walt grinned sheepishly. He was pleased. He liked Joe, almost like a son. He wished he saw more of him, as well as of Jack, but he didn't because Peg didn't like Joe and always nagged him if he saw Joe, and he kind of thought that she shouldn't see too much of Joe and Dorothy, lest Joe think Dorothy's family was interfering. He remembered how Peg's family always used to interfere in his life. God, sometimes he even thought that Peg was like her mother. And her mother had sure been one hell cat. But he liked Joe. He was a good, regular young fellow, and he was good to Dorothy. He was pleased by the way Joe and Jack talked to him, and he didn't see why he and Joe and Jack couldn't kind of pal around some. But he didn't know how Peg would take it.

"Maybe I'll take up bowling again next winter," Walt said.

Peg frowned at him. Well, he didn't care if she liked it or not, next winter he'd go bowling with Jack and Joe.

I I

Watching his grandchildren, Walt thought again of Jack and Dorothy when they were young. Golly, they'd been cute. But Dorothy's boy, little Willie, and Jack's girl, Marie, they were cute, too. Willie was five and Marie was four. And Dorothy's and Joe's one-year-old girl, Catherine, was in the crib. She was as sweet as any baby he'd ever seen. He really liked kids, and it was wonderful to be a grandfather. From now on he was going to see more of his grandkids. Willie and Marie had been out running in the yard, and now they were pulling little toys and talking, and then they were silent with the Lord knew what going on in their little minds. He enjoyed just watching them. And he was thinking, too, how he had worked to raise Jack and Dorothy, and now they had their own children and were raising them, and that was something. It was something to leave happy kids and grandchildren after you. It made you proud and made you feel that living and hard work were worthwhile. And it just melted you sometimes when they called you "Grandpa."

Peg had gone up to little Willie and asked him to talk to her.

"I don't want to."

"But why? Little boys should like their grandmothers."

"I don't want to."

"But why don't you want to talk to your grandmother?"

"Because I don't like to."

This conversation had hurt him, because he could see that it had hurt Peg. Hell, he didn't want to hurt her, even though it seemed she often did things that hurt others, and certainly she said and did things that hurt him.

Dorothy hadn't liked it and had told Willie to talk to his grandmother. But Joe hadn't seemed to mind.

"Listen," Joe said, "he talks like that to me. The day before yesterday he said to me, he asks me: 'Say, who do you think you are?'" Joe laughed good-naturedly, and there was pride in his voice. "So I says, 'A hell of a lot more than you. I'm your old man.'"

Peg was quiet now, sitting in the corner as if she had been crushed. It made Walt nervous to see her that way. But he didn't know what to say or do about it; he hadn't done anything to cause it, and she couldn't say he had.

Now Willie was in front of him.

"Grandpa."

Walt leaned forward, and a soft look came into his eyes.

"Yes, Willie," he said.

"Grandpa. Give me a piggy-back ride."

"Sure, I will."

"He's too old to do that. It might affect his heart," Peg said.

"Yes, Willie, don't ask Grandpa to do that. Maybe he can do something else for you. Maybe he can tell you a story," Dorothy said.

"I can do it," Walt said.

"If you get sick and have a heart attack, I'll have to take care of you. But don't say I didn't warn you," Peg said to him.

"I'm all right . . . dear."

Walt had hesitated a moment before calling her "dear," and he knew he hadn't wanted to call her that.

"All right, Willie, your grandfather'll give you a piggy-back ride," Walt said, getting out of his chair.

But as he bent down he had a sudden fear that maybe he oughtn't to do it. He wished Peg hadn't spoken.

"Hold on tight, now," Walt said after his grandson had climbed onto his back.

"I will."

The babyish tones of the boy's voice touched him.

Children talked with such innocent voices, he thought to himself.

He slowly rose to his feet and, grinning, jogged out of the parlor with his laughing grandson on his back.

Peg was morosely silent.

I I I

The children had eaten separately. Dorothy and Peg had set the table and helped Maggie finish the cooking. Peg had been somewhat in the way, wanting to do things her way, and there'd almost been a scene between her and Maggie. Peg had kept telling Maggie how hard it was to cook a Sunday dinner for a big family, and that she shouldn't have bothered to invite Walt and her over until after they'd eaten. Maggie had assured her mother-in-law that it had been no trouble at all, but Peg had continued to talk of how much trouble it was.

Now the table was spread with food—roast beef and mashed potatoes, vegetables and salad—and Maggie had used the dishes Walt and Peg had given them as a wedding present, dishes she liked and prized, with country scenes on the plates. The sight of the food seemed to cheer up everyone except Peg. Seeing all the food, Walt knew he was hungry and said:

"My grandchildren gave me a good workout and worked up my appetite."

"I warned you, Walt, don't say I didn't, if you have aches and pains tonight," Peg said from across the table.

"Oh, nothing like that is going to happen," Walt told her. "I didn't overdo myself."

"I don't know where children get all their energy. At the end of a day I'm often good for nothing," Dorothy said.

"Oh, you're pretty good for something along about bedtime. Ha! Ha! You better be," Joe said.

"You better be, too," Dorothy retorted.

Peg frowned. At first Walt wished Dorothy and Joe hadn't talked that way, but then he thought it was the way a man and his wife should be about it when they loved each other, and he wished it had been like that in his own marriage.

Joe carved the meat and, after putting some on each plate, passed the plate down to Dorothy. She piled potatoes and vegetables on. Soon they all had heaping plates in front of them and began to eat. They ate more than they talked, and for a while there was only intermittent and casual conversation.

"Now, back in the Depression you couldn't stow away grub like this," Joe said.

"I hope we never have to go through another time like that," Walt said.

"You didn't suffer," Peg told him.

"I know—knock on wood. I held my job. Some of the Supervision was put back on the trucks, and a few of them never were brought back. There is one fellow, Willie Collins. He was a Dispatcher, but they put him on a truck, and it's pathetic. Every time I see him he talks about when they're going to put him back in Supervision. And there was a good friend of mine, Simon Murray, he was put on a truck, too. He only retired last year, but his pension ain't enough for him to live on, so he has a job now as a night watchman. And a lot of men were laid off. I'll never forget those times, and I don't want to see them again. Speaking for myself, I'm glad I was able to put bread on the table for my family every day."

Walt moved everyone at the table but Peg. He had spoken with rising feeling. He was proud that he had kept want away from the door of his home back in those days when so many men were out of work, and he was proud that ever since he was married he had never been out of a job.

"As a matter of fact, I haven't been out of work since the day I was married," he went on. He was really talking for Peg's benefit, trying to tell her that he had done his best.

"Well, Walt, I'll knock on wood myself. I've worked steady since Dotty and I were hitched up."

"Yes, Joe, you've been every bit as good a provider as Daddy here," Dorothy said.

"But I sure was on my uppers many times before that."

"You were able to keep your job because Patsy McLaughlin had respect for me," Peg said to Walt.

Her remark came as a surprise to everyone.

"He kept you on as a Wagon Dispatcher during the Depression because I met him and his wife at the wake of one of your expressmen, and they liked me."

"Patsy died before the Depression. I remember that, and I remember it well. Because I saw the Cubs play a couple of times that year, and they had Rogers Hornsby and won the pennant that year, and I remember it because I was talking about it with someone at Patsy's wake, God have mercy on his soul."

"Well, then out of consideration for me he must have left instructions to keep you on," Peg said.

For a moment Joe stared at Peg as if he thought she wasn't all there. But Dorothy looked at him anxiously, and after she caught his eye he shrugged his shoulders.

"I don't regret it, but I think I can say it in front of my own children, Walt Callahan—I helped you in many ways. It's me who gave you backbone. When I married you, you were a teamster."

"Mother, we know you did. And Father knows, too," Dorothy said, trying to check her mother and to appease her at the same time.

Walt was embarrassed. He was worried that Joe and Jack might think him a mollycoddle and might even pity or laugh at him.

"Peg, you can work and clean a house better than me, but I can make a living and do my job at the Express Company," he said.

"Hell, you think Dotty there could run a lathe like I do?" Joe said. "We got dames at our shop. They work a little while, and what happens? They're off sick. Or when the foreman comes around, they're breaking their necks workin', workin' us out of a job. They'll do too much for three days, and the foreman will be on our tails. Then what happens? They're off sick again."

"Men can't bear the pain that a woman does. I'd like to see any man having a baby," Peg said.

"Peg, that's something you're never going to see on God's green earth," Joe said.

Walt took another helping of food from Dorothy. He really didn't want to eat any more, but he went ahead, even though he felt he was doing something he oughtn't. And yet there was nothing wrong with eating a good, hearty meal, was there? Then, having eaten too much, he felt heavy and bloated and began to belch at the table.

I V

It was mighty pleasant to be sitting out here after dinner and smoke a cigar and be near the grandchildren, sort of watching them and half-listening to them, but at the same time having your own thoughts. And he was proud to think that Jack owned this little house and was paying for it, and it was his, his and Maggie's. Jack was a smart young fellow, and he was doing fine as a salesman. Funny, Jack being a good salesman, because he didn't act like a lad with the gift of gab. And he had a garden, too, and kept it neat, and that must give him satisfaction. He might have done all kinds of things himself if Peg hadn't put her foot down on his suggestions. Peg didn't want them to own a home. That time they went looking on a Sunday afternoon, she was so against it that he gave up. And he just let it go since she felt that way. God, seeing Maggie here and his daughter as a wife, it made him realize how different they were from Peg. Like cooking dinner. Maggie and Dorothy didn't complain or talk about it being so hard or of being tired, and, well, they did things so different from Peg. And Jack and Joe were happier husbands than he was, or than he guessed he'd been even when he was their age.

"Grandpa, she won't play," Willie said, coming up to him.

"Why?"

"She won't," Willie said, indignant.

Marie ran up to him.

"I won't. I won't," she said in childish petulance.

"Now, what won't you do, little lady?"

"I won't play that I get shot all of the time. Why can't he get shot?"

"Because she's got to be the Japanese and I got to be the American."

"Can't you take turns?"

"Yes, Grandpa. But . . . "

Willie stopped.

"He says grandma is like the Japanese and I got to be like her and be shot."

Walt cast a hasty glance toward the kitchen door on his right. God, if Peg heard this.

"That isn't nice, to speak like that of your Grandmother," Walt said in a low voice.

"I don't like her," Marie said.

"She loves both of you. She loves you very much."

"No she doesn't."

"Who told you that?"

"She looks like this all the time," Willie said, making a long face.

"She never plays with me. You do. We love you, Grandpa," Marie said.

"You should love her because she loves you and your mother and father," Walt said.

He looked anxiously at the kitchen door again. He didn't want Peg to overhear any of this. She'd blame him, and he'd never hear the end of it.

"Why don't you play another game—tag, for instance."

"He always catches me, and I can't catch him. He's a boy," Marie said.

"You can't be a boy," Willie told Marie.

"Yes I can."

"No you can't."

"I can too."

Marie turned to her grandfather.

"Grandpa, who made me a girl?"

"God did."

"I want to be a bad boy."

Walt laughed.

Willie ran off shouting. Marie chased after him, and soon the two children were digging in a corner.

Walt puffed on his cigar. He was saddened by what his two grandchildren had said of Peg, and he remembered her, young and beautiful, holding Jack as an infant and singing *Rockaby, Baby*. He'd been happy then sometimes. She'd taken good care of Jack and Dorothy, and he remembered her playing with them and often reading them stories at night in the days when she hadn't been nervous and cranky. Gosh, he'd thought her such a good mother then. And Peg washing diapers and getting up early in the mornings to give them their bottles. And staying up all night when the kids had pneumonia. He could remember lots of things about Peg besides her temper, and he could remember loving her, and their hopes for the kids, and, God, now the kids were grown up and he and Peg were old, but they were kids to be proud of. And why shouldn't she be proud, too?

He didn't know. He didn't understand it at all.

"Grandpa! Grandpa!" Willie shouted, running to him, with Marie following.

He felt great love for the two youngsters as he waited for them to come to him.

"We dug a hole. Come and see it."

Willie and Marie grabbed his hands. He let them pull him up while pretending to read.

"Gosh, you're strong," he told them.

Still holding his hand and chattering rapidly, they led him to the hole.

V

"You sit down and rest and I'll do the dishes," Peg said in the kitchen.

"No, Mother, you go and sit down. I'll do them," Maggie said.

"Maggie and I can do the dishes, Mother. Why don't you go out and sit with Father and the kids?" Dorothy said.

"I get headaches in the sun," Peg said.

"I have a big old straw hat I can let you put on," Maggie said.

"You cooked and set the table. I'll do the dishes and give you a rest."

"I can do the dishes," Maggie insisted.

"You don't have to worry about me, I'll get them clean. I always rinse them well, very well, to get the soap off. You don't have to worry, Maggie, about my not getting the dishes clean."

Maggie stared at her mother-in-law for a moment, surprised.

"Why, I know that, Mother," she said quickly. "but I don't ask my guests to do my dishes."

"I'm family," Peg said.

"Mother, you did plenty of work in your day. Now you should take it easier," Dorothy said.

Ignoring Dorothy's remark, Peg started for the sink.

"You girls go and talk to your husbands, and I'll do the dishes," she said aggressively.

Maggie stepped in front of her at the sink and said quietly but insistently:

"Mother, I'm doing the dishes. You can dry them with Dorothy if you want to."

Peg stared at her daughter-in-law, but Maggie met the stare. Then Peg looked off, smiled meekly, and turned to Dorothy.

"Give me that dish towel, Dorothy."

Maggie started washing the dishes. She and Dorothy talked proudly of their children. Peg listlessly dried the dishes and showed no interest in the conversation.

"Look at him," Peg said suddenly, pointing at the window. "Look at him down on his hands and knees, digging with the children."

Dorothy and Maggie gazed out the window and saw Walt digging with his grandchildren.

"He's having a good time, Mother. He loves to be with the children," Dorothy said.

Peg froze up and went on drying the dishes.

V I

"Father could enjoy life and his old age more if Mother could. It's sad—sad that Mother can't enjoy life more," Dorothy said.

She was sitting at the dining-room table with Maggie, Joe, and Jack, having coffee. The baby was asleep, and the other two children were upstairs playing quietly. It was dark out, and they were all relaxed.

"I hope I didn't hurt her feelings," Maggie said, looking at Jack with uncertainty.

Jack was silent.

"Maggie, it wasn't your fault. When Mother comes to my house and wants to do things and help me, it's the same—it's more trouble than it's worth," Dorothy said.

"She makes me nervous. I guess every woman has her own way of doing things, and her way is different from mine. But it's more than that—she just makes me nervous. And it's the same when my own mother is here to a family dinner. I don't want my mother to wash all those dishes."

"I like my mother, but I don't want her making any trouble or getting in your hair, Maggie," Jack finally said.

Maggie smiled at him.

"Father looked well—and he had a good time. I could see he did. He loved playing with the kids," Dorothy said.

"Yeh," Jack said thoughtfully.

"The old fellow looked pretty good," Joe said.

"And he told me that one of the big shots at the Express Company likes him and that maybe one of these days he'll get a promotion. Gee, I hope he does. He deserves it," Dorothy said.

"I'll have to take in a ball game with him. I used to get a kick out of going to games with him when I was a kid," Jack said, a note of nostalgia coming into his voice.

"Oh, he was good to us when we were kids."

"He was a grand old man," Jack said.

"You know, he never hit us much. Mother would more than he, but she was a good mother, too. She did lots for us. I feel sorry for her. Even when we were kids she couldn't get much pleasure out of us." Dorothy laughed. "I guess we were devils, though. I was a tomboy."

"I know. You always wanted to tag around with me," Jack said.

"And you were ashamed of me because I was a girl," Dorothy said.

"Hell, when you're a kid, you don't want girls around."

"Jack," Joe said, laughing, "they're still tagging after us. You go in a tavern, there's a dame. You go in a barber shop, there's a dame gettin' her hair cut short or something—"

"Yes, and you don't like it," Dorothy teased.

"Who says I don't?" Joe asked.

"You're not like Father in that way—he never chased skirts," Dorothy teased.

"Yeh, and with all due respects to your old lady, don't get like her," Joe said.

"I wanted to talk to her but I didn't know what to say—I didn't," Jack said.

"If you get as nervous as Mother, you can't enjoy life. She gets me mad sometimes—and I don't want to get mad at her and fight with her. When I do, I feel awful afterwards," Dorothy said.

"I always try to be friendly with her, but I wouldn't go into her kitchen and insist on doing things if she told me not to," Maggie said.

"I remember she was always worried and making a fuss about our coming in the kitchen with dirty shoes," Jack said.

"She looked so unhappy today, I wonder what we can do for her," Dorothy said. "I worry and think about her a lot. But when I see her, then it all starts again, and she tells me about Father. I love him. I love her, too. But I know Father, and I know she's wrong and ought to act different with him."

"He's henpecked," Jack said.

"I don't henpeck you, Jack," Maggie said.

"You know my feelin', Maggie. A man's work is his business. A woman's is the home. You run the home. I make the dough," Jack said.

Joe yawned.

"We'll have to be going," Dorothy said.

"Don't you want more coffee or another beer before you go?" Maggie asked.

"I could drink a bottle of beer," Joe said.

"Jack?"

"No, dear."

Maggie got Joe a bottle of beer and poured some in his glass.

"I just wish I could do something for Mother," Dorothy said. "Every time I think of her or see her, it makes me sad and worries me."

"Me, too," Jack said. "Hell, I'd do anything I could for her and Dad. But they don't need money. Dad earns a good salary. I don't know what I can do except tell her to take it easy, and if you say that to her . . . " Jack shook his head from side to side. "It doesn't do any good."

"Yes, and it breaks my heart sometimes when I see her; you know, she's really aged."

"Yes, she doesn't look too well," Joe said.

"You know, Mother was beautiful when she was young," Dorothy said.

"Yeh, I seen pictures of her," Joe said.

"And I have one picture of her when she was Marie's age. She looked like a darling little girl. She was a beautiful child. Oh, it makes me so sad."

They all became moody and said nothing for several moments.

Then Jack yawned.

"Joe, you'd better finish your beer. We've got to wake Catherine up and get her and Willie home and to bed," Dorothy said.

"Okay," Joe said, yawning too.

They all yawned.

"Well, folks, thank you for such a wonderful dinner and a grand day."

"We liked it," Maggie said.

"And it gave the old man a good time," Jack said.

"I like him so much," Maggie said warmly.

Joe nodded. He finished his beer and got up to go.

V I I

"Today was a nice day. I enjoyed myself," Walt said, chuckling. "Peg, we got some mighty fine grand-children, and two good kids, too, in Dorothy and Jack."

It was about nine o'clock, and they'd just gotten home. Walt felt sluggish. He was sorry they'd left so early, but Peg had wanted to, and so here he was. The day was over, and this was one day he hated to see end. It had been one of those days when a man was so happy he was sad. He felt good. Yes, it did his heart good to be with his kids and grandkids, and with Joe and Maggie. They'd all acted as if they loved him, and they made him feel he was somebody. And he was somebody to them, too.

But now, with the day over and Peg and himself back home, he only felt lonelier. And Peg hadn't seemed to have a good time. She had been so silent and had seemed so unhappy and so angry, it made him feel he'd done something wrong. He hadn't done anything wrong, except maybe overeat.

He guessed it was best not to say anything to Peg but just to wait and see if she'd come out of feeling whatever it was she felt, or maybe say she was tired and go to bed without saying anything to him or blaming him. But sitting here and saying nothing and not knowing why Peg looked so angry and unhappy, well, it made him nervous. He had to say something, even though he kind of thought keeping quiet was the best thing for him to do.

"Yes, it was a nice family get-together," he said, hoping Peg would agree with him.

"Joe is a brute. I don't know why Dorothy married him. What did she ever see in a man like him?"

"They seem to be happy, and Joe treats her nice. I don't see anything wrong with Joe."

"How could a brute treat a woman the way she should be treated? And how could you know if a man's a good husband? You—you aren't a husband."

"Peg, I've always tried to be a good husband, I have," Walt said earnestly.

Suddenly he remembered how, when he'd been younger—oh, it must have been back when he'd been in his forties—he'd often wanted another woman, and had even wanted to go to a whorehouse, but he hadn't. He wanted to tell Peg this, but he was afraid to. Maybe it wasn't fair of him to wish it, but he wished he had done it. Hell, he just felt hurt and all mixed up. He wished she'd stop. He didn't want any more arguments. That was all.

"He never looks at a woman. Why, he might just as well have married a home as a woman, just the way you did," Peg said in denunciatory tones.

"But, Peg, he is a decent, hard-workin' fellow. He is. I've seen many who spend their money on booze and beat their wives and chase skirts, and Joe doesn't."

Walt knew that he should keep his mouth shut.

Peg nervously began to pace the floor, wringing her hands as she did. She gave him the jitters again. What was the matter with her, he asked himself earnestly.

"What a show you were today—you, a grandfather!"

"Why, the children seemed to like me. I got along fine with them."

"You're not even ashamed of yourself. You're an old man, and you haven't even a sense of shame."

"Peg, what kind of talk is this?"

"Oh, the sight of you with your gray hairs and your fat face!"

He looked at her graying hair. And his face wasn't fat, either.

She strode out of the room. Seeing his kids today happy and married, he realized that things didn't have to be the way they were with him and Peg. And it was getting worse and worse. He'd wanted it to be different. Oh, God, this had been going on for years, and he had kept hoping that it would stop, that Peg would change. And all the while he seemed to have known that it wouldn't. Now, at his age, he had to admit that his life was just full of hell, yes, hell, and that as long as Peg lived it would go on being the same, go on being just full of hell.

He became stiff with fear and looked anxiously to

the back of the house. But he hadn't done anything. Everybody died. God, strange thoughts came to a man.

He lit a cigarette out of his need to relax, to do something.

Now she was coming back. What would she say? She had a glass of beer in her hand.

A sulky expression crossed his face. He hadn't asked for a glass of beer.

"I don't want no beer," he said petulantly.

"Here it is. I got it for you. Don't tell my children and my son-in-law and my daughter-in-law and my grandchildren, the way you did today, that I don't take care of you. Don't talk about me the way you did to Maggie."

"I didn't say nothing like that about you to Maggie or any of the others, Peg," he said.

"I know what you said. And, oh, what a fool you are—not seeing what she's doing to your son."

"Why, Jack and Maggie love each other, Peg."

"Love?" she asked vehemently.

"I didn't see anything wrong between them, Peg."

"You wouldn't. You wouldn't understand that she hates my son because she hates me."

"Peg, please—"

"You like it. You'd see Jack and the whole world ruined just to get at me."

Walt shook his head as if he were groggy.

"Well, now you know that I know your game."

"What game, Peg?"

"Your game."

"I'm not playing any game, Peg. I'm trying to live my last years in peace and to support and take care of you and myself . . . Peg."

"Drink your beer and don't tell them that I don't hop to your call."

"But I didn't—"

"I ought to be called your bellhop instead of your wife," she interrupted.

"But I didn't—"

"No man ever talked against his wife the way you talked against me today, Walter Callahan."

"But I didn't say—"

"Then why was my own flesh and blood so mean to me today—it would wring the hardest heart."

"But they didn't treat you bad—they love you and they treated us both swell."

Why didn't he keep still now? He didn't want this to go on.

"Swell—yes, Maggie practically told me to get out of her kitchen. And all I was doing was offering to help her."

"What did she say? I didn't hear it."

"No, you didn't. You just told them lies about me, and I was insulted. I'll never darken their doors again."

"Peg, I don't know what you're talkin' about. Honest, I don't."

"Now you have the boldness to tell me to my face that you didn't run me down and talk against me."

"But, Peg, I didn't say—"

"They know—my son and daughter know. They hate you. They don't hate me. I'm their mother. They know, Walter Callahan. They hate you. They don't hate me, and you didn't blacken me and my name to them. The horse manure you flung at me didn't hit me. But you've talked to Joe and Maggie. And they don't know—they don't know, and they were mean to me because they're playing your dirty game. You know, Walt Callahan—"

"Peg, please—"

"Admit it!"

"I ain't done nothing to admit."

She gave him a look of contempt and swept out of the room.

V I I I

It was about ten o'clock. Peg was screaming at him. He felt as if he were sick. It was worse than feeling sick. It was feeling sick in your mind and in your heart. She had called him so many names and said so many things to him that hurt—yes, they did.

And she wouldn't stop screaming. The neighbors must hear her, and, God, what would they think? It made him ashamed. The things she said and shouted and accused him of weren't true, and, by God, he knew they weren't. And here she was, still shouting and screaming and cursing him. He couldn't think.

He couldn't sit quiet and hear all this. He was just damned fed up with the way Peg treated him and talked to him and carried on, and he wasn't going to sit here like a dummy.

"Goddamn you, shut up! Shut up right now!" he shouted at her as he sprang to his feet.

Peg cowered. She looked at him suspiciously, like a little girl fearfully and carefully studying the face of an adult.

"You've talked too goddamned much already."

Her lips quivered. Beads of perspiration broke out on her forehead.

"I'm fed up with your goddamned talk. Not a goddamned word of it is true, and you know damned well that it isn't, and I know damned well it isn't."

"You're cruel to me."

"Well, then, why don't you cut it out and let me alone?"

"No man ever talked to a woman the way you talk to me."

"Talk to you—Jesus Christ, don't pull any sob stuff on me now."

Her lips were trembling and her eyes showed fright. She looked as though she were trapped. For a moment he felt pity for her. But, goddamn it, she jawed and yapped at him and nagged at him until he didn't know if he was coming or going or spinning around like a crazy top. He was going to have it out with her now and settle a thing or two.

Then Peg gave him a meek look, turned, and sat

down. She fixed sad eyes on him and said nothing.

"What do you get out of nagging me, throwing all of this goddamned crap at me? What do you get out of it?" he asked in anger.

She did not answer him. She merely sat looking desolate, fixing sad eyes on him.

"Does it make you happy?"

Peg sobbed.

"Now you're going to cry and carry on as if I had beat you. Now we're going to have tears as if I did something to you."

Peg's body shook with sobs. Again, Walt was touched. He felt that he was acting rotten with her. But he knew how she had jawed and jawed him. He had all the memories of her nagging, and he couldn't stop. He had to make her understand, once and for all, that she had to change her nagging tunes.

"What the hell are you crying for?"

She went on sobbing.

"What did I do to you to make you cry?"

She wiped her eyes and looked at him helplessly. His arms dropped awkwardly to his side, and he merely stared at her, hurt and bewildered. He realized that after all the years he'd been living with her he didn't know her.

I X

The beginning of another week. God, how many Monday mornings of his life had he not ridden to work, beginning a new week of work to earn money for his family? Years and years of Monday mornings. And never in all these years of Monday mornings had he felt quite as he did on this Monday morning. And what did he really feel? It was, well, it was different from anything else he had felt. It was . . . well, it was hopelessness. That's what it was. He didn't know what to say about Peg, except that as far as he was concerned it was all just hopelessness. He couldn't look forward to any joy and peace, to growing old, to going slowly down the other side of the hill, to walking slowly down the big slope in sunshine and contentment. That was what he couldn't feel. That was what he couldn't look forward to. And a man like him who had worked all of his life and wasn't an educated man or a rich man or a famous man couldn't look forward to anything in life if he couldn't look forward to that. That's why what he felt was hopelessness.

And feeling hopelessness like this only made him more sad about the times when he and Peg were young and happy together. He couldn't remember those days now the way you should remember good times in the past. Now it hurt too much to think of when he had been so much in love with her and had come home to her and the children, feeling he was building a home and a life, and feeling . . . well, feeling happy. It hurt too much now to remember all of that.

But why? Why? What had happened to Peg to make her act the way she did?

The car was crowded, as it always was in the mornings, and Walt hadn't gotten a seat. He hardly had slept at all last night because of the way Peg had acted. But still he wasn't tired. He'd thought almost all night. He'd lain in bed beside Peg and he'd thought. There she had been asleep. She had been asleep and had forgotten it all, forgotten their life together in her sleep, but he had not been able to do that because of thoughts of hopelessness. He'd been sore, but it was something more than being sore. Yesterday, last night, when they'd come home from Jack's and she'd carried on and he'd bawled her out —yesterday and last night had done something to him.

Because of Peg he'd often gone to work feeling rotten, feeling plenty rotten. And yet this morning it was different. He felt rotten, plenty rotten this morning, hanging onto a strap, being jolted, with workingmen shoving and bumping against him, but he felt more than that. Because now he knew something. Now he knew what he should have known for a long time. Now he knew that it was no use, no use whatsoever. Hell, he'd felt good when he'd bawled Peg out. No, he guessed he'd just thought he felt good, just kidded himself with a feeling that he didn't really have. She had cried and just folded up, and she had given him peace then, but what kind of peace?

Hell, he guessed he felt sorry for himself. It was like coming to know that you were an old man, that life was pretty much over for you. And Peg? She was old, too, and he felt sorry for her. God, the last thing in the world he wanted to do to her was to talk to her the way he had last night. But he had to, because she wouldn't let him alone, she wouldn't let up on him. He felt sorry for her, but there was a limit.

And now here he was riding to work and thinking again of everything he'd thought of last night in bed.

Some of the men in the car were sleepy. A workingman near him looked as if he were only half awake. On many of the faces there was a look of patience. Did he have that kind of look on his face? It was the only way a man could feel going to work early in the morning, only half awake, and especially on a Monday morning. But a lot of them on this car were young fellows. They had a long way to go before they would ever add up the years of Monday mornings that he had ridden to work in streetcars. And he guessed they were going to work after a night of loving up their wives. Hell, he'd gone to work like that after having loved up Peg the night before. It was hard to believe this now, but it was true. It had happened to him long ago. But it was hard to remember nights like that and to remember what it had been like, and what it had felt like. It was all over. Most things in his life were all over. What was he to do but to go on like this? Maybe he should have known it and understood it before, but, anyway, he hadn't. Until last night and this morning, he hadn't come to understand that he could never expect Peg to change or be different from what she was, and it was a damned bitter pill to swallow.

The streetcar was starting and stopping, starting again, jolting the passengers. A few of them were talking, but most of them were just sitting or standing, as patiently as Walt. There were a few women and girls in the car, but none of them were near him. What were they like, and were the older ones better off than Peg or not, having to go to work at this hour of the morning when she could sleep late and didn't have much housework to do, not too much, and had her time all to herself for most of the day? God, what did Peg do with herself all day?

The jammed streetcar, jolting along on the sunny morning, going a little faster, slowing down, stopping, starting up again. The motorman clanging the bell, the conductor ringing the signal bell to start again after each stop, and Walt thinking, asking himself what Peg did with herself in the daytime, and feeling a hopelessness that he believed he had never felt before, and then beginning to wonder what life was like to all these other people in the car, wondering if any of these other men felt as he did and had wives like Peg. And then, as the car once again came to a stop, Walt asked himself:

—What do you do to be happy and to have a happy home?

X

Walt at least had his work. She had nothing. Day after day, she had nothing to do. If she was working, even if she was scrubbing floors in some office building, she'd have something to do and she would be independent. She would be earning her own pay, and she wouldn't be the servant and slave of a man. A man? No, of a brute, a horse who looked like a man and who talked in neighs. He brought home his pay check to humiliate her. Her life was one of humiliation. At her son's home yesterday he had humiliated her. And she had nothing to do. All she had to do was to keep the stable for him. And would he be happier in this stable if she tied a bag of oats around his head at night and let him eat it and put straw on the floor? Oh, she had no life.

Sitting slumped in Walt's chair, with a sad and empty look on her face, she drearily said to herself:

—No life! No life! No life!

—I have no life!

—No life! No life! No . . .

—I never had any life, no life!

And how could the horse understand it, how could he?

A wild look came into her eyes, and she began to neigh aloud. She tightened up as she neighed, hunched her shoulders, and then a thrill bordering on ecstasy ran through her body. For a moment she felt an extraordinary and strange sense of freedom, as though she were not herself. She neighed more loudly, and she seemed to hear herself neighing as though she were someone else.

She got to her feet and let out a new succession of loud, wild neighs. She got down on her hands and knees and crawled around the room, and then she got to her feet, neighed once, and sank back into Walt's chair, limp and wearied and with her hair disheveled. She sat slumped in the chair, drained of energy, looking old, her face pale, wan, lined, her eyes sunken behind hollowing, wrinkled ridges, focussing on nothing, her hands clasped, and her elbows pressed against her ribs. Then her body sagged as though the energy had flowed out of it.

"Horsey, horsey," she said in a cracked, tired, whispering voice. "Horsey, horsey, Walt's too old to play horsey, horsey, horsey."

She sat slumped for a long time, with a fixed, wild stare in her dark eyes.

X I

Peg was very nervous, restless, at loose ends with herself. She didn't know how the morning and early afternoon had passed. She had the strangest feeling that she had been somewhere else today, somewhere far away from this miserable home of hers, but she didn't know where. Something had happened to her, but she couldn't remember what. And she was terrified because of this. She couldn't remember. She knew that she hadn't been bad, and yet she felt as though she had been very bad and had done something she wouldn't want a single soul in this whole world to know about.

And now the day was passing. It was getting late, and she hadn't done her housework. If she didn't hurry up, she wouldn't get it done before he came home, and he'd bawl her out. He was always bawling her out, the way he'd done, so cruelly, last night. He had no right to treat her the way he did and expect her, at her age, and after all she'd done for him, to go on slaving for him. He couldn't expect her to be a horse.

She was overcome with a strange feeling of terror again. She sank back into Walt's chair and cowered with fear. She shook, waiting in a paralyzing dread for something to happen to her from moment to moment.

Her mind went black, and she sat for some moments. Then she suddenly got up and began to clean the flat with a furious nervous energy.

X I I

Just as he went to work and would go to work for
some years yet, if his health didn't fail him, so would
he be coming home from work for some years to
come, just as he was on this Monday afternoon. And
for what? All day, he had been depressed. He
couldn't shake off his mood. He couldn't forget Peg.
He couldn't kid himself or fool himself or pull the
wool over his eyes any longer. He couldn't convince
himself that there was any use, because he knew now
that it was just no use, and that it would never be
any use. It didn't do him a damned bit of good to
hope about himself and Peg. And it was knowing
this and feeling it as if it was in his blood and bones
that made him feel that there was no hope at all.
God, he was like a man trying to walk with his feet
tied in a potato sack, or trying to hammer a nail
handcuffed, or trying to walk blindfolded.

Yes, here he was at the end of another day's work,
going home, riding over the old familiar route again,
and he didn't want to do it, he didn't want to go
home, he didn't want to see Peg and sit down to supper with her and talk to her and go to bed and sleep
beside her. He didn't want to do it. He wanted to go
away and start life all over again. But he was too old
to do that. What young woman would want him?
What kind of a job could he get? Yet Porky Mulroy
had done it, and who would ever have thought that

Porky could, fat as he was—hell, Porky was fat as a pig. Porky had done it. But, then, Porky had been younger when he walked out and must have had more spunk than he had.

No, he just didn't have spirit to do it now, at his age.

An evening newspaper was jammed in his coat pocket. He couldn't read it. He didn't care what had happened today in the world. He wasn't interested in what other people had said and done. If he tried to read his paper, he would read the words all right, but the words wouldn't make any sense to him. He'd just read without knowing what he read. That was the way he was this afternoon.

He looked about him on the streetcar, and the men and women he saw seemed strange to him. He felt as though he had a weakness they didn't have, and that they might even be able to sense and know of this weakness and criticize him for it. And his weakness was that all of these years he'd put up with Peg and hadn't known. But what hadn't he known? He hadn't known . . . known what? Known that it was no use and that you couldn't be happy with her or have any kind of life with her? No, he hadn't known that she was the way she was. And these men and women on the streetcar, they must have some kind of life and get some kick out of life. Thank God, his kids did. And at least there were some men he worked with who did. Heinie Mueller, now, he'd gotten some kick out of his life. Young Casey did.

Hell, Casey wasn't young any more. Time had passed. He was getting old. He'd been riding here on streetcars like this for years, and during that time he had started to get old. He was getting old now, and here he was riding home again, and to what? How would she act tonight? Would she give him any peace? Would she be complaining?

He clutched the strap. The car swayed and jolted. He asked himself:

—Christ, what is the use?

X I I I

When Walt entered the apartment, he was too low to want to talk or even to say hello to Peg. But he spoke anyway.

"Hello, Peg."

She didn't answer. She stared at him as if she didn't even see him, and she looked so sad and unhappy that he didn't want to be near her.

"Is anything the matter, Peg? Did anything happen? Are you all right?" he asked, very concerned.

Again she didn't answer. Her gaze was fixed, but she didn't seem to be looking at him or seeing him. God, she gave him the creeps. Just to see her this way made him afraid. He didn't know what to do. He didn't know what to say.

"Peg—Peg, what's the matter?"

She laughed strangely, as he'd never heard her laugh before.

He went toward her, and she tensed up and sprang to her feet.

"Peg, come on, what the devil is the matter?" he asked, and as he spoke he put his hands on her shoulders.

She shuddered. Her entire body trembled and quivered with fear. She screamed.

Walt jerked his hands away from her, drew back, and gaped at her, shocked. It seemed to him that something dangerous had happened to him or would happen to him at any moment. There she stood in the middle of the living room, staring at him with a fishy-eyed look.

He opened his mouth to speak but said nothing. He didn't know what to say.

Still not knowing what to do, he took off his coat and went to the bedroom to hang it in the closet.

"Hey, what's this," he yelled in surprise.

He found two suits of his clothes cut up, ripped, and scattered all about the floor. He leaned down and picked up scraps of his blue serge suit and examined them. He was too bewildered to say anything or even to think. He stood, blank-faced. Then he began examining the shreds of his destroyed suits. And his new gray suit, too. My God, was the woman out of her head?

"Peg," he called.

There was no answer.

He rushed out of the room. She was still sitting mute in his chair in the parlor. He went to her.

"Peg, what in the name of God's the idea? What happened to you? Peg, Peg! Peg, have you gone out of your mind?"

She whimpered.

"Goddamn it, you ruined my two best suits of clothes. I paid sixty dollars apiece for them suits. Are you out of your mind, woman?"

She seemed to be very far away from him.

"Answer me? What did you do that for?"

"They told me to," she intoned in a flat voice. "They told me to. They told, told, cold, cold . . ."

She lapsed into silence again and became almost immobile.

Walt's anger collapsed. His shoulders sagged. His arms hung at his side. He looked at her, wounded and hurt. He left the room, went to the bedroom, sat on the bed, and gazed blankly at the ruins of his two suits. He turned, lay down on the bed, and his body suddenly shook with sobs.

X I V

Peg sat listening to the voices she heard. The voices told her:

—He'll kill you.

Her eyes came alive, flashed. She stealthily removed her shoes and then drew a carving knife from her blouse. She rose and walked out of the room on tiptoe, with a trancelike expression on her face.

Walt lay still on the bed, feeling drained and humiliated. He thought he heard a soft movement. He thought he sensed someone in the room. He didn't move for a few moments.

As if she were still in a trance, Peg came across the small bedroom with the carving knife poised over her head. As Walt swung around, she stabbed and caught him in the throat. Blood gurgled out, and he made an effort to rise but fell back on the bed. Then Peg withdrew the knife and stabbed him over and over again.

X V

Walt lay dead. His corpse, the bed, the floor were splattered with blood. Her hands and dress sticky with blood, Peg sat by the bed with a wild, mad look in her eyes. Her lips moved, and she mumbled to herself. She sat for a long time, and the house grew dark as she became silent and immobile by the corpse of her husband.

—I must cook Walt's supper, she suddenly told herself.

She rose, walked out of the room, went to the kitchen, switched on the light, and began to cook the evening meal.